"I Want Whatever You're Able To Give Me."

Hesitating a moment, Shannon added, "For however long it lasts."

"If you knew what was good for you, you'd take off running right about now."

She cradled his strong jaw in the palm of her hand. "I don't need to run," she murmured softly. "You are very, very good for me, Mr. Lancaster."

His fingers trembled against the soft skin of her cheeks. "I wish I could give you everything you deserve."

"What is it you think I deserve?" she asked gently.

"Forever," he ground out hoarsely. "You deserve forever, Shannon."

"No one can guarantee forever, Donovan."

"Most men could give you a sincere commitment, but I can't."

"Can't or won't, Donovan?"

The laugh he uttered then was a cynical burst of sound that sliced into Shannon and left her torn and bleeding inside. "I won't," he admitted curtly.

Dear Reader,

This month we have a very special treat in store for you. It's the Silhouette Desire "Premiere" author for 1993! This is a completely new, never-before-published writer, who we have chosen as someone exciting and outstanding. Her name is Carol Devine, and her book is *Beauty and the Beastmaster*. There is a letter in it from her to all of you, her new fans. *Who* is the Beauty and just who—or what—is the Beastmaster? Well, I'm not telling; you'll have to read and find out.

In addition to our "Premiere" author, October has five more favorites. Our *Man of the Month* is from the delightful Cait London. The lineup is completed with wonderful books by Jackie Merritt, Christine Rimmer, Noelle Berry McCue and Shawna Delacorte.

As for *next* month . . . it's a winner! We've decided to "Heat Up Your Winter" with six of our most sensuous, most spectacular authors: Ann Major, Dixie Browning, Barbara Boswell, Robin Elliott, Mary Lynn Baxter and Lass Small. Silhouette Desire . . . you just can't get *any* better than this.

All the best,

Lucia Macro
Senior Editor

NOELLE BERRY McCUE
MOONLIGHT DREAM

SILHOUETTE *Desire*®

Published by Silhouette Books New York

America's Publisher of Contemporary Romance

SILHOUETTE BOOKS
300 East 42nd St., New York, N.Y. 10017

MOONLIGHT DREAM

Copyright © 1993 by Noelle Berry McCue

All rights reserved. Except for use in any review, the reproduction or utilization of this work in whole or in part in any form by any electronic, mechanical or other means, now known or hereafter invented, including xerography, photocopying and recording, or in any information storage or retrieval system, is forbidden without the permission of the publisher, Silhouette Books, 300 E. 42nd St., New York, N.Y. 10017

ISBN: 0-373-05815-2

First Silhouette Books printing October 1993

All the characters in this book have no existence outside the imagination of the author and have no relation whatsoever to anyone bearing the same name or names. They are not even distantly inspired by any individual known or unknown to the author, and all incidents are pure invention.

® and ™:Trademarks used with authorization. Trademarks indicated with ® are registered in the United States Patent and Trademark Office, the Canada Trade Mark Office and in other countries.

Printed in the U.S.A.

NOELLE BERRY McCUE

who helped launch the Silhouette Desire line under the pseudonym Nicole Monet, lives in California. "I've always loved to read," the author says, "and writing has filled a void in me I was never consciously aware of having. It has added depth to my life and a greater awareness and appreciation of the people around me. With every book I write, I hope I am in some small way paying for the pleasure that reading has given me over the years. If I can help just one person find enjoyment and release from everyday troubles, then I've accomplished my purpose in my chosen field."

The author concludes by saying, "That's why I write romances—because they leave the reader with a positive attitude toward love, life and relationships. When all is said and done, isn't it love for others that gives us the greatest happiness in life?"

To Dot and Bud Heiser,
the best godparents anyone could have.
All my love,
Noelle

One

Donovan Lancaster stood with one shoulder propped against the frame of the doorway that separated his best friend's living room and family room. As he watched the party going on around him, he ran a hand through his thick, overly long, dark blond hair. Twin slashes of silver at his temples added distinction to the informal style.

His manner and choice of clothing were usually as casual as his haircut, but this morning he had dressed in a black suit and tie. A pristine white dress shirt gave his craggy, broad-featured face prominence, and at the moment there was a slight frown compressing his mouth. Tiny lines fanned out beside a pair of catlike eyes, attesting to every one of his forty-two years.

Those eyes were a deep, darkly golden brown in hue, and there was an intriguing slant at each corner of his thickly lashed eyelids as he stared at his surroundings with brooding restlessness. The cool green-and-blue decor, which showed occasional splashes of rich cream, was soothing, as well as elegant. Donovan, much to his increasing irritation, felt anything but soothed.

With pensive, absentminded attention, he swirled the glass he held in a circular motion and shifted his position restlessly. Lifting the cool rim of the glass to his lips, he sipped at the watered-down Scotch and grimaced. He rarely drank, but at the moment he was bored, edgy, and in a foul mood because there was so much he had left undone at home.

Several years ago he had turned the huge Piedmont, California, estate he had inherited into a shelter for teenage runaways, and keeping the place operating smoothly was a never-ending task. He knew the staff he employed were perfectly able to deal with most contingencies, but he liked to be on hand whenever possible. He wasn't a man who could delegate responsibility with an easy mind—which wasn't much of a virtue, he thought, considering how often his temper suffered as a result.

Or, to be more accurate, he amended with inward amusement, how often others had to suffer his temper as a result. Right about now he should be on the phone with the retail merchants who regularly donated funds to the shelter, or balancing the books, or overseeing the unloading of the produce trucks due to arrive today. Yet he could hardly have refused to show up at a function given to celebrate the christening of his friend Drew's three-month-old daughter, especially when he had been asked to be little Tina Michelle's godfather.

He and Andrew Sinclair went back a long way, he mused, remembering a shy blond youth and his pesky little sister, Tricia. Those two had given him the kind of innocent, unquestioning affection he had never received from the stern, demanding grandfather who'd raised him. Drew had been a rather spindly ten-year-old when he started following Donovan around, while Tricia had still been in diapers. As a superior fifteen-year-old, Donovan had been amused and a bit flattered by Drew's obvious hero worship.

Donovan's thoughts turned to the ceremony that had been held a few hours before, and he shook his head in amazement at how much had changed since those long-ago days. Drew no longer had any reason to emulate him. He was a successful lawyer with a wife and baby he adored, while his old friend was still a proud, hardheaded rebel who walked a lonely path by choice. Yet at times like this, Donovan found himself contemplating how different his life might have been if he had married and had children of his own.

A tender light entered his eyes as he pictured his goddaughter in his mind. He had carried Tina up to bed a short while ago, and had spent several minutes just watching her as the guest of honor enjoyed the sleep of innocence. Her predominantly bald head, with its tiny topknot of black curls, had nestled against a white satin pillow while the adults who had set aside this bright September day to share in one of the first big moments in her life celebrated.

Donovan was not enjoying the festivities, however. In fact, he was as taut as a bowstring, and he knew damn good and well why. He hadn't planned on returning to Drew and Maria's place after the ceremony, not with all the work waiting for him at the shelter. Yet here he was in living color, he realized in disgust, standing around with all the stomach-curling anticipation of a kid waiting in line for a visit with Santa Claus.

Although he would have liked to think he was dutifully fulfilling his role as godfather, he had to admit that his presence had nothing to do with his new responsibilities, and everything to do with the little green-eyed redhead he had been introduced to on the church steps this morning. He inhaled sharply at the memory. The smile she had given him had taken his breath away, and he was still having trouble getting it back.

Staring into Ms. Shannon Dalton's thickly lashed emerald eyes had been his first mistake; touching her, his second. When he'd grasped the hand she extended to him, he had felt every sane thought fly right out of his head. He hadn't even responded to her politely murmured greeting, he recalled now with belated embarrassment. Instead, he had nodded curtly and scowled at her like an ill-mannered oaf, too stunned by the swift, hot surge of desire he was experiencing to stifle his instinctive defensiveness.

A slight commotion in the entry hall had his eyes swiveling in that direction, and his hand tightened around his glass when the subject of his thoughts strolled into view. He studied her slender figure through narrowed, contemplative eyes, and wondered what there was about her to attract him to this extent. She was pretty, in a wholesome, fresh-faced way, but her looks were unexceptional. And she was so tiny!

A weak breeze would probably knock her off her feet, and he doubted the top of her fiery head would reach the middle of his chest. He favored statuesque women who could measure up to his broad six-foot-plus frame, he told himself, but even the derisive reminder failed to assure him of his continued preference for long-haired brunettes and svelte blondes. Much to his dismay, he still couldn't seem to take his eyes off this particular female.

He snorted in self-disgust. She was little more than a pixie-faced moppet with a riot of close-cropped red-gold curls—so what was it about her that fascinated him to this extent? He didn't know, and that was what disturbed him most of all. Her figure certainly wasn't anything to write home about. His taste ran to full breasts and rounded hips, he thought in near desperation, not to a petite female who wouldn't weigh much more than a toy poodle.

So why, when she obviously wasn't his type, was he getting all hot and bothered? Judging by appearances, she was the quintessential girl next door, he decided, and as such, she was a lousy candidate for an affair. Her kind of female expected commitment, and all that word entailed, while he preferred to run free and unencumbered. Yet there was no denying the attraction he felt toward her, he realized uneasily, when even the freckles sprinkled across her pert little nose turned him on!

He watched Shannon pause to converse briefly with her host and hostess, and then step down onto the cream-and-green-flecked living room carpet. Her soft voice barely reached him, and yet he found the low, husky murmur sweet enough and melodious enough to blend with angels at prayer. Unable to control his thoughts, he began to imagine those dark, honeyed tones whispering to him under the cover of darkness.

His chest tightened at the erotic image his active mind conjured up, an image of a perfect bow of a mouth breathing endearments against his passion-moistened flesh as she lay curled on top of his naked body. That particular erotic fantasy was far from angelic, he decided sardonically, but it was most definitely stimulating. He didn't even know this woman, and yet there was no doubt in his mind that he wanted her with an obsessiveness he found extremely disturbing.

But that was nothing compared with the anxiety Donovan experienced a moment later, when he saw Drew's sister heading in Shannon's direction with a decisive stride. For the past year or so, Tricia's sole purpose in life seemed to have been matchmaking, and a large portion of her time had been spent trying to provide him with suitable matrimonial candidates. He could argue his preference for bachelorhood until the cows came home, he decided glumly, but Tricia would do little more than smile, ignore him and introduce him to yet another member of the fairer sex. When he suddenly remembered that Shannon Dalton's cousin, with whom she was visiting, was one of Tricia's best friends, his heart continued to sink, until it reached the same level as his shiny black shoes.

It took all of Shannon's willpower to prevent herself from glancing around the crowded room in search of the man she had met that morning. She didn't know why he should have such an impact on her, but there was no denying it. She had never before experienced such an overwhelming, instantaneous attraction, not even toward the man she had once been engaged to marry. Those golden eyes of Donovan Lancaster's had pierced through her defenses with the force of a laser beam, seeming to burn a message on her senses with no appreciable effort.

Of course, the attraction had been entirely one-sided, she assured herself, trying to feel relieved instead of disappointed. In fact, if his expression had been any indication of his feelings, Mr. Lancaster had taken an instant and quite inexplicable dislike to her. He had certainly frowned at her ferociously enough, she recalled, repressing an urge to sigh with a despondency quite alien to a woman who scorned the indulgence of self-pity.

She really didn't care if she ever saw the unpleasant man again, she told herself firmly, squaring her shoulders. She thanked her host and hostess for their hospitality and wandered toward the living room. Keeping her seeking eyes firmly under control, she decided against following her cousin Debra and her family as they gravitated toward a group of their friends. She had had all the introductions she could handle for the moment, and she wanted to find a quiet corner to hide in for a while.

Unfortunately, there was no way she could hide from the thoughts that continued to attack her conscience. That wasn't surprising, however. She had trained long and hard to establish a career as a critical care neonatal nurse, and she had sacrificed a great deal for her advanced education. Yet here she was, her heart and mind in turmoil as she tried to decide whether or not to abandon her specialized area of medicine.

If only she hadn't been laid low by that damned pneumonia virus, Shannon thought irritably, she wouldn't have had the time to start doubting the future she had always envisioned for herself. She loved children, and none so much as the babies she struggled, sometimes futilely, to save. The tiny, helpless ones, without even enough strength to cry in protest at the rotten hand they had been dealt. The ones who were tinier than the dolls she had played with as a little girl, and so pitifully, heartbreakingly frail.

She was losing her objectivity, and the stress she was subjecting herself to on a daily basis was taking its toll on her emotional and physical well-being. She knew it, and her doctor knew it, and yet acknowledging the situation in no way helped to alleviate the problem. Which was why, when Debra had invited her to visit the Bay Area, she had jumped at the chance to escape her usual surroundings for a while.

Her illness had done more than force her to slow down and reassess her priorities, she decided. It had also made her face some unpalatable truths about herself. She wasn't invincible; nor was she content with her lot. Her demanding career had merely formed protective scar tissue over a very old wound. It was a wound she had suppressed so stringently it had never been allowed to heal, she realized now.

Her thoughts were wrenched backward to the day of her premarital exam, when the doctor had plastered a benign smile on his face and muttered something about a "slight irregularity." A series of tests had followed, and she had been devastated to learn that her tubes were malformed and it would be extremely difficult for her to conceive a child in the normal manner. Her fiancé had seemed to take the news well, and had even discussed alternate methods of conception with the doctor.

That was why she had been stunned when he broke off their engagement several months later, confessing that he wanted to marry someone else. Discovering that he'd been seeing another woman had been bad enough, she remembered, but she had been devastated to learn that his new love interest was pregnant. She had found herself wondering bitterly if he had started cheating on her before the doctor's verdict, or after. Not that it had mattered either way. Her confidence in herself as an attractive, desirable female had been shattered, and from then on she had pushed her personal needs into the background of her life and concentrated on her career.

Yet more and more of late she had been realizing that she wanted something from life other than a career and financial security in her old age. She was trying to believe that there was more to Shannon Dalton than a starched uniform and a pair of skilled hands. Her slowly growing confidence in herself as a woman was comforting, as well as surprising, and she wondered when she had stopped punishing herself for something she hadn't been able to help.

Not for the first time, she asked herself if this impromptu visit wasn't a mistake. In her preoccupied state of mind, she wasn't the best choice as a houseguest, and she found it rather difficult to observe even the simplest of social amenities. She had mentioned as much to Debra last night, in an attempt to get out of attending today's festivities, but that no-nonsense individual had soon set her straight.

"Sitting here trying to rack your brain for answers you don't have isn't going to serve any useful purpose," Debra insisted. "What you need is something to take your mind off your troubles."

Shannon gave a sigh that seemed to come from the depths of her soul, conceding that Debra was right. She didn't have any answers, and brooding about her situation wasn't going to provide her with any sudden revelations. She would just take one day at a time, she decided staunchly, and hope that eventually she would get her act together.

The crowd around her appeared to be thickening, and she was on the verge of claustrophobia when she decided to head for a large potted palm in the far corner of the room. All she wanted to do at the moment was sit quietly, and indulge in a little people watching. It was a favorite pastime of hers, and maybe it would provide her with the distraction she needed.

She had taken no more than a couple of steps when she found her path blocked by a tall, elegant blonde in a lovely rose silk sheath. "You must be Debra Harrison's cousin Shannon," the other woman remarked, holding out her hand with a warm smile. "I'm Tricia Everett, a friend of Deb's."

"Oh, yes!" Shannon exclaimed with pleasure, clasping Tricia's hand firmly. "Debra's mentioned you often in her letters. You're also my host's sister, aren't you?"

Tricia nodded her elegantly coiffed head. "The very same, much to Drew's continued bewilderment. He's convinced that Mother found me under a thornbush, and brought me home just to torment him."

Shannon chuckled with rueful understanding. She had two older brothers of her own. "I've been looking forward to meeting you, Tricia."

"That goes double for me," Tricia admitted with a widening grin. "Deb hasn't talked about anything but your visit for days, and my curiosity's been killing me."

Shannon grimaced with embarrassment. "In other words, she's been boring you to death."

The younger woman's delicate bone structure and porcelain-perfect complexion gave a Madonna-like serenity to her features, but Shannon couldn't miss the mischievousness in her impishly dancing blue eyes. "A conversation with Deb is never boring. She's better at ferreting information out of people than I am, and as a psychologist I consider myself something of an expert."

Shannon chuckled, and waved her hand in an expansive gesture. "Ask away," she offered, surprised by how much at ease she felt with this woman. "My life is pretty much an open book, especially with a cousin like Debra."

"I envy you that." At Shannon's questioning look, she said, "Both my parents were only children. I always wondered what it would be like to have aunts and uncles and cousins."

"Well, I have dozens of them." A single dimple indented the left corner of Shannon's mouth, and her eyes sparkled with suppressed amusement. "The Daltons and Mahoneys are a formidable clan, and I'm the youngest of four myself. Although I've never married, my brothers and sister are continuing the tradition in style. Between them, they have quite a brood."

Although her response was teasing, there was a curious intensity in Tricia Everett's eyes as she asked, "You're not antimarriage, are you?"

"Not at all," Shannon replied quietly. "I was engaged once, but the relationship didn't work out. Since then I haven't met anyone interesting enough to get serious about."

"Oh, that's all right, then!"

Although somewhat confused as to the reason for Tricia's relieved exclamation, Shannon shrugged aside a vague, niggling unease and tried to change the direction of the conversation. "Spoiling nieces and nephews is quite an art, you know," she said. "Now that you're an auntie, feel free to ask my advice anytime."

Bright blue eyes widened in mock horror. "Don't let my sister-in-law hear you say that. She's already threatened to hang me up by my ears if I add one more stuffed animal to her daughter's collection.

"Not that I pay any attention to her," Tricia added with cheeky insouciance. "Maria was my best friend before she married my brother, and there are still a few stunts we pulled in our riotous youth that she wouldn't want Drew to find out about."

"Ah, blackmail..." Shannon drawled with suppressed humor. "I bet you and my cousin get along famously. Deb got me into more trouble in my teens than my brothers and sister managed to get into put together. I think that's why I graduated from high school with grades that earned me a college scholarship. I was stuck in my room on restriction so often, there wasn't much else to do *but* study."

Just then they were jostled by a passing guest. As though of one mind, she and Tricia headed for a bow-fronted window embrasure that had just been vacated. As they seated themselves on a cushioned bench seat, Tricia crossed her slender, silk-clad legs and emitted a relieved sigh. "My feet are killing me."

Shannon eyed her own stylish footwear with disfavor. "I know what you mean. I'm used to spending long hours on my feet, but not in these high-heeled monsters."

"That's right, you're a nurse," Tricia remarked. "I remember Debra telling me you primarily deal with critically ill infants."

Shannon nodded. "I work in the neonatal unit of L.A. General. Or I did, until a bad bout with pneumonia brought me down."

Tricia winced. "I caught the virus myself a few years back, and for two weeks I could hardly get out of bed. Even after I was over the worst, it was quite a while before I stopped feeling dragged-out and listless."

"It did take me a bit longer than I'd counted on to recover, but I'm finally back to normal."

"Oh, then I guess you'll be reporting back to work soon," Tricia remarked with visible disappointment. "I was hoping you'd be staying long enough for us to get to know each other."

"Actually, I won't be returning to the hospital for several months," Shannon said, with a forced smile and a shrug. "I . . . have some personal stuff to work through, so I decided to take an extended leave of absence. Actually, I'm not sure if nursing really is for me."

The other woman clearly saw through Shannon's casual demeanor, and she frowned in concern. "If there's anything I can do to help, just let me know."

"You wouldn't happen to have a solution for terminal boredom, would you? I've been a workaholic for too many years to take so much leisure time in my stride."

"You remind me of Maria," Tricia said with a laugh. "Once she founded the Family Assistance Center for Emergency Shelter, there was no stopping her. She worked full-time as an apartment manager for my husband, Marcus, and all of her spare time went to FACES. It's a wonder Drew ever pinned her down long enough to get her to marry him, let alone to conceive my niece."

A sudden idea leaped into Shannon's mind, and she wondered why she hadn't thought of it before. "That's right, I could tag along with Debra when she goes to work. A stint as a FACES volunteer would be the perfect way to keep my brains from atrophying."

"Oh, you don't want to do that!"

Shannon blinked in surprise at the other woman's dismayed exclamation. "I don't?"

"I have a much better idea," Tricia insisted. "Can you cook?"

"My mother taught me the basics, and I slung hamburgers at a fast-food place for a few months when I was in college." It hadn't been one of Shannon's favorite jobs, so her response was cautious. "Why?"

Instead of answering, Tricia leaned toward her with subdued eagerness. "Since you chose to work in a neonatal unit, you must like children. How are you with teenagers, Shannon?"

Puzzled by this intense line of questioning, Shannon searched Tricia's animated features uneasily. "I get along great with my teenage nieces and nephews, if that's what you're asking."

At that admission, an odd look crossed Tricia's face. "You're perfect," she muttered beneath her breath. "Just perfect!"

Shannon studied the golden-haired beauty's animated features, her uneasiness growing to gigantic proportions. "I beg your pardon?"

Instead of answering, Tricia quickly surveyed the people who had almost filled every inch of space in the living room. Apparently her searching glance found its mark, because she clasped Shannon by the hand and began dragging her through the crowd. "There's someone I'd like you to meet," she flung breathlessly over her shoulder. "You two have a great deal in common."

"Uh-oh," Shannon mumbled, thinking she knew how a lamb must feel on its way to the slaughterhouse. She should have recognized that matchmaking gleam in those guileless blue eyes, she realized with a sinking sensation in the pit of her stomach. Lord knew she'd seen it often enough among the members of her own family. She was probably going to be presented to an over-the-hill widower with twelve kids, and it was all her own fault. One of these days she was going to learn to keep her big mouth shut!

She had never wished that more fervently than she did in the next instant, when Tricia stopped in front of the one man in the room most guaranteed to make her tongue-tied. It was the sandy-haired Viking with the sexy, heavy-lidded eyes. At the moment, those light brown orbs were studying the snug fit of her powder blue crepe de chine dress, seeming especially interested in the modestly rounded neckline and the pleated bodice.

Resisting the urge to cross her arms over her chest, she stammered, "Mr. Lancaster and I have already met, Tricia."

Mr. Lancaster failed to respond one way or another. He seemed flatteringly reluctant to lift his gaze to her face, which was surprising considering the smallness of her blessings in the particular area holding his attention. But, fortunately, Tricia chose that moment to clear her throat, and both Shannon and Donovan started nervously before turning to stare at her in confusion.

"Well!" Tricia glanced from one to the other with obvious satisfaction. "Ummm...I guess I don't have to perform an introduction, then."

"No," Donovan said, eyeing his best friend's sister with overt suspicion.

"No," blurted Shannon, bewildered by the sudden evident tension in a body masculine enough to weaken her knees and rattle her bones.

"Donovan has been like another brother to me, Shannon," Tricia prattled on with dogged persistence and a fixed smile. "I always had Drew right where I wanted him, but this guy was another matter entirely. He was patient with my youthful tantrums, but he didn't let me get away with much. If the truth be told, he was probably the person responsible for preventing me from turning into a holy terror in my youth."

"That's a matter of opinion," her savior muttered cynically.

If the *real* truth be told, Donovan had known that Tricia spelled trouble before her eighth birthday. She had been a female version of Dennis the Menace, he remembered with what he considered irrational fondness, complete with flyaway blond hair and an angelic smile. A zest for adventure, combined with a vivid imagination, had tended to land her in some kind of jam with alarming frequency. As far as he was concerned, nothing much had changed over the years.

She had even rushed into marriage with a rough-edged tycoon both he and Drew had disapproved of. But Donovan would be the first to admit that Marcus Everett had proved to be a settling influence on his wife. Now, if only the duo would begin to produce offspring of their own, he thought with a familiar twinge of exasperation, he might be able to breathe a little easier.

He doubted it, though. If anyone was a born match-maker, it was this golden-haired, blue-eyed thorn in his side. Still, he hoped that if she had a baby or two to fuss over she would be too busy to continue trying to find him a suitable wife. And maybe pigs would grow wings, he decided with grudging resignation. If he knew her, he would still be trip-ping over her matrimonial candidates when he was well into old age.

Tricia's smile faltered a bit at the dirty look she was re-ceiving from Donovan, but she continued with her praise of the tall, scowling man with plodding determination. "You might not know to look at him, Shannon, but this guy has a real soft spot for kids."

Donovan's scowl deepened, his chiseled mouth com-pressing into a sternly forbidding line as he stared at Tricia. Shannon glanced up at him and wondered how such a hard-looking man could possibly possess any soft spots. Catch-ing sight of her doubtful expression, Tricia gritted her teeth and glared at Donovan as if she'd like to kick him in the shins. "It's true, Shannon," she continued on a note of desperation. "I assure you that beneath this stonelike fa-cade of his there beats the heart of a pussycat."

Two

The pussycat retaliated with a subdued roar. "The heart of a what?"

Shannon winced. The air around them seemed to vibrate, but apparently Tricia Everett wasn't the type of woman to be cowed by the indignant bristling of a mere male. Maybe she hadn't been able to wrap Donovan around her pinky finger as she had her brother, Shannon thought with amused certainty, but she was obviously secure enough in his affections to ignore his disapproval with admirable panache.

Seconds later, the other woman proved her right by gesturing expansively toward Shannon, her expression smug. "I have the solution to your most recent problem, Donovan."

The innocent comment triggered a salacious vision in his mind, one of a small, perfect body as naked as the day it had come into the world. He saw a tangle of red-gold curls lying on a plaid pillowcase, and a pair of big green eyes looking up at him. His pillowcase . . . his bed . . . and the eyes of a temptress beguiling him with the promise of heated passion.

All at once, the throbbing that had started in his loins the instant Shannon walked into the room became more than a minor irritation on the fringe of his thoughts. Indeed, it became a potential for embarrassment. His brain fogging as his heart rate increased, he stammered stupidly, "W-what problem?"

Tricia gave him a rather disconcerted look, which rapidly disintegrated into one of impatience. "The one you mentioned the other day. You said your cook and her fiancé upped their wedding date and headed for Reno, right?"

Instantly alarmed, Shannon blurted, "Tricia, I don't really . . ."

"Right." Donovan snapped the word out with a tightly locked jaw, not at all worried about polite behavior. "What are you getting at, Bubbles?"

When she heard the hated childhood nickname, Tricia glared at him, and emitted an unladylike sniff through her classically perfect nose. Her eyes glittered like twin jewels with razor-sharp facets. "Shannon has some cooking experience."

"Short-order," Shannon croaked weakly.

She might as well have saved her breath, because what little she had left whooshed out of her lungs when Donovan fixed her with an unwavering stare. But eventually his attention shifted, and he continued to question Tricia. "I thought she was vacationing?"

Although she didn't much like being talked about as if she were a stick of furniture, Shannon had to admit that she felt a cowardly relief at Donovan Lancaster's preoccupation. But her relief was brief, because all too soon his eyes once again zeroed in on her. "Aren't you?"

The question was barked at her so suddenly that she gasped, and jumped like a frightened mouse. "Well, in a manner of speaking, I..."

Without waiting for her to complete her sentence, Donovan leveled a triumphant glance at Tricia. "There, you see? Ms. Dalton wouldn't want to screw up her vacation plans."

Resentful at being cut off so abruptly, Shannon's head angled back stiffly as she sought to put him in his place. "I didn't say that, Mr. Lancaster."

His chiseled mouth firmed in annoyance. "Then what are you saying?"

She didn't know, and that made her more provoked with him than ever. She was about ready to suggest that he take his cooking job and shove it up his arrogant nose when Tricia beat her to the punch. "You don't have to badger her to death, Donovan. Shannon was very ill recently, and she decided to take an extended leave from work."

Tricia made it sound as if she had been at death's door, and Shannon nearly groaned aloud when a pair of piercing eyes once again headed her way. "What's wrong with you?"

Shannon heard the note of concern in his gruff voice, but his manner further fired her temper. "Nothing," she replied stiffly. "I went a couple of rounds with pneumonia a few weeks ago, that's all. I assure you, I'm fully recovered."

Studying the militant angle of that pert little chin, Donovan decided he didn't hold out much hope for the survival of any poor, battered germs. He was forced to compress his lips to hide a grin at the thought. Still, her confidently aggressive behavior failed to reassure him as to the state of her health. "Then why haven't you returned to work?"

"Did I mention that Shannon's a nurse, Donovan?" Tricia offered in an attempt to lighten the tension developing between the two of them. When only silence greeted that golden tidbit of information, she resorted to more desperate measures. "A pediatric nurse, and she's great with teenagers."

Since the exaggeration seemed to have little to do with the conversation, Shannon let it pass. She was too busy deciding how to respond to this unpleasant man's last question. "I've worked my tail off for several years, and I decided a break was in order. Do you have something against rest and relaxation, Mr. Lancaster?"

Arching a brow quizzically, he stated flatly, "So Tricia was wrong, and you're not interested in working for me?"

Feeling backed into a corner, Shannon shifted her gaze from him to the dejected figure standing beside him. "Well, not exactly. I haven't been actively looking for a job, but I..."

Tricia placed a hand on her arm, her expression apologetic. "I didn't mean to put you on the spot, Shannon. You mentioned being bored, and I just assumed that a job with Donovan would be welcome. I'm sorry if I've embarrassed you."

Shannon was quick to reassure the crestfallen woman. "You haven't, but I really don't think..."

"Ha! You're not alone!" Donovan gestured toward Tricia, his tone exasperated. "This is one female who's famous for acting first and thinking later."

"I am not!" the female in question retorted with a petulant frown. "Anyway, the point is that Shannon's available and you need a cook. It's a match made in heaven."

It was definitely the wrong choice of words. Donovan's face reflected all the dark beauty of a thundercloud ready to dump its load on the unwary. "Don't think I'm oblivious to what's really going down here, Bubbles. Your subtlety leaves a lot to be desired."

Tricia's head took on a defiant tilt. "So sue me!"

Shannon was nothing if not wary. "Listen, you two, you really don't have to..."

By now quite accustomed to being ignored, Shannon let her words trail off as she glanced from Donovan Lancaster to Tricia Everett and back again. They were standing practically nose to nose, their eyes locked together as unspoken messages seemed to zing between them with dizzying force. It was a battle of wills between two forceful personalities, and Shannon stared in silent admiration as she tried to guess which of them would emerge the victor.

Donovan was wondering much the same thing himself. Trish was on a roll, which didn't bode well for his powers of resistance. He had never placed her on the pedestal her brother had, he thought, but he hadn't been far off the mark. She had learned to bat those long eyelashes of hers when she was little more than an infant, and he was no more immune to soulfully reproachful looks than any other poor sap. Especially since he knew that her interference in his life was based on genuine concern and affection.

That weakness was never more apparent than in the next instant, when Tricia stood on tiptoe to land a repentant kiss on his cheek. "Stop scowling, Donovan," she said softly, "or Shannon might think you don't want her."

Donovan froze at the reprimand, his gaze sharpening on that angel-innocent face. He tried to decide whether her choice of words was accidental, or whether the remark had held an underlying innuendo. But Tricia was giving nothing away, he realized in defeat. Her wide eyes were as guileless as a suckling babe's. His annoyance increasing the longer he studied her bland expression, he glanced away in frustration.

Unfortunately, his gaze landed on Shannon, and that proved to be disastrous. His heart began to hammer inside his chest, and he was sent reeling by an awareness of his own vulnerability. A whiff of the perfume she was wearing drifted in his direction, and his body tightened in heated reaction. His chest rose and fell on a muffled sigh. He was completely enveloped by her scent.

The floral fragrance reminded him of a dew-drenched field of violets, but what really sent his mind spinning was the clean, damnably sensual essence that was pure woman. His hands tightened into fists as he acknowledged the strength of his attraction to her, and he promptly broke out in a cold sweat. Since he was all too conversant with the betraying signs of the initial stages of arousal, he did his best to hide his reaction from Tricia.

Although he had certainly been acting like one, he was no fool, especially where that little minx was concerned. If she ever guessed at the full extent of his attraction to her newest matchmaking prospect, there'd be hell to pay. There probably would be anyway, he decided grimly. And what really stuck in his craw was the knowledge that he only had himself to blame!

If he hadn't played the gallant knight when her own marriage was stagnating from her husband's lack of attention, Tricia wouldn't have felt she needed to pay back the favor. Since then, she had been expounding on the benefits of matrimony to him every chance she got, ad nauseam. It was almost more than a man could take.

Tricia had convinced herself that he was miserable as a bachelor, and no amount of protesting on his part was going to change her mind. The trouble was, the stubborn woman was a dyed-in-the-wool romantic. Since she always saw the world through rose-colored spectacles, she would probably even view his lust-at-first-sight reaction to Shannon as an encouraging sign.

He finally managed to untangle his frozen vocal cords with some semblance of rationality. Still, when he spoke, his voice was much less forceful than he'd intended. "I'll only need a cook for two weeks, but the position is full-time," he reminded Tricia. "Ms. Dalton might not want to tie herself up to that extent."

Swiveling gracefully on her sling-back heels, Tricia started belting out questions in a manner that would have done the

Spanish Inquisition proud. "What do you think, Shannon? It's already mid-September, and I don't know how long you were planning to visit the Bay Area. Can you work at the shelter through the end of the month?"

Shannon snuck a glance at Donovan out of the corner of her eye. When she noticed the grim cast of his lips, her spirits plummeted. As she had suspected when they met, this man was not at all well-disposed toward her. She wondered if he objected to her personally, or if he was just a common, garden-variety misogynist. The thought was a distressing one, and she quickly glanced away to prevent him seeing the disappointment clouding her eyes.

Shrugging her shoulders in a gesture of unconcern, she replied to Tricia's question with little enthusiasm. "I'm not due back at the hospital until January second, and I'm in no particular rush to get home."

"You see?" Tricia crowed triumphantly. "Why should you bother hiring a temp when Shannon's available?"

Donovan was being backed into a corner, and he definitely didn't like the sense of helplessness he felt. Out of all the people at the FACES meeting the other night, he groaned inwardly, why had he chosen Tricia as a confidante? He must have been out of his ever-loving mind, blabbing about his troubles to a born busybody.

Yet his irritation wasn't really aimed at Tricia, but at himself. His preoccupation with Shannon must be causing his brain to deteriorate. He had already interviewed two perfectly suitable candidates for the shelter's kitchen. If he'd kept his wits about him, he could have stopped this argument before it got started by simply opening his mouth and telling them the position had been filled.

Donovan knew himself to be a decisive man, even a stubbornly willful one at times. He was definitely a man who liked calling the shots, especially when in pursuit of a woman. There was no way he was going to allow himself to be manipulated. Absolutely no way! Squaring his shoulders, much in the manner of a soldier mentally girding himself for battle, he studied Shannon's apprehensive face and hardened his heart.

His mouth opened. "The job's still available if you're interested."

Shannon offered him a timid smile, briefly puzzled by the conflicting emotions she saw reflected on his craggy features. The tight compression of his lips denoted annoyance, but she couldn't tell whether it was aimed at her or at her vociferous champion. His eyebrows were scrunched together, and yet his frown seemed to convey more confusion than anger. And if she wasn't mistaken, his eyes held a rather glazed, shocked expression in their depths.

Her searching glance stopped at those beautiful golden eyes, and as she held his gaze his expression altered with a suddenness that nearly caused her knees to buckle. It was most assuredly not the look a man gave a woman he found unattractive, and that certainty caused her entire body to tingle with escalating excitement. Nervously moistening her lips with the tip of her tongue, she gave him a tentative smile. "This conversation has been rather confusing, but I gather you have need of a cook, Mr. Lancaster."

Donovan's fascinated gaze followed the path of that small pink tongue, and he thought of another, more urgent need he'd like her to satisfy at her earliest convenience. Suddenly finding it difficult to swallow, he cleared his throat before replying to her question. Even then, he was able to manage only a gritty-sounding "Yes."

"Where is your restaurant located?" she asked.

He stared at her blankly. "My what?"

"You don't own a restaurant?"

When he shook his head, her even white teeth began to nibble on the lip she'd just bathed with moisture. "Is . . . is the position in your home, then? Will I be working for your wife?"

Although she had slipped the latter enquiry into the conversation with apparent unconcern, Donovan felt a surge of satisfaction. If she wasn't interested in more than a job, he thought, then why should she wonder about the possible existence of a wife? He just barely managed to keep his expression calm as he replied, "Yes and no, and I'm not married."

Some of Shannon's tension was eased by his reply, but confusion quickly took precedence over relief. "Yes and no?"

"I run a shelter for teens at my estate in Piedmont, which is located in the hills above Oakland."

Her eyes were round with surprise. "I thought that area was destroyed by fire."

"Much of it was, but, by the grace of God, the fire storm bypassed us."

Donovan's eyes darkened as he recalled fighting an enemy that at times had seemed unconquerable. The experience had been as close as he cared to get to hell on earth. Quickly shaking off the terrible memories, he said, "The shelter houses about fifty people when it's full, and you'd be responsible for feeding them. Still interested?"

Although she was somewhat nonplussed by the enormity of the task he had just described, she was intrigued by the idea of working at a shelter for runaway teens. She would be too busy to brood over her uncertain future, that was for certain. And she had always enjoyed helping her mother and aunts prepare food for their yearly family reunion, which was a formidable task. She could handle the work—she knew she could!

Yet a sense of fair play made her hesitate to commit herself. This man had been backed into a corner, and she needed to be certain he really wanted her to work for him. "You don't really know anything about me."

"I'll take my chances."

She deliberately held his gaze. "I might be a terrible cook."

"As long as there's plenty, hungry kids don't tend to be too critical."

Once more biting down on her lower lip, she said, "Mr. Lancaster, I..."

"Donovan," he said softly.

His eyes settled unswervingly on her piquant features, and he was oddly touched by her hesitant manner toward him. His chest rose as he drew in a deep breath, and he hurriedly stuffed his hands in his pockets as he fought an urge to wrap his arms around her in a reassuring hug. He didn't want to give her the impression he was a lecher, even if he felt like one whenever he looked at her.

If she guessed he had seduction on his mind, she would probably turn tail and head for home at top speed. If that happened, he would probably never see her again. Just the thought of her disappearing before he had a chance to explore these strange, overpowering feelings she generated inside him caused him to flinch inwardly and gaze at her delicate features with compulsive thoroughness.

A delighted Tricia saw that look, and she murmured a smugly complacent goodbye as she drifted off, doubtless looking for another challenge. Neither Shannon nor Donovan noticed her departure. He was holding his breath as he waited to hear whether Shannon would agree to work for him, and she was too dazzled by his tawny eyes to do more than stare at him like an idiot. Yet in spite of her preoccupation, Shannon intuitively sensed that she was at a crossroads, and that a single misstep might spell disaster.

"Well?" Donovan muttered suddenly, as impatience overcame the sensuous spell threatening to disable his tongue permanently. "Are you interested in the job?"

Shannon sailed past the crossroads without a backward glance, her eyes sparkling. "I'm interested, Mr. Lan—"

"Donovan," he said, interrupting her.

His slow smile curled her toes. Shannon was unaware of how tenderly her mouth formed his name as she repeated, "Donovan."

But he was aware of it, and hot blood surged in his veins. "And may I call you Shannon?"

The huskily voiced question made her feel as shy and awkward as a teenager, and she flushed in embarrassment at her gaucheness. "Of—of course you may."

"I'm going to have to take off in a few minutes, but would you have dinner with me tomorrow night?"

Misinterpreting her surprise as hesitation, he was quick to add, "If you haven't already made plans, that is. It would give you a chance to see the shelter, and we could discuss any questions you might have while we eat. Say about six o'clock?"

His logical attitude should have reassured her, but she felt a shocking sense of disappointment at his businesslike manner. What was happening here? she wondered uncertainly. This man was reaching inside her and tugging at strings she hadn't been aware of possessing, and she was confused by the strength of the emotions he was arousing. She would do well to keep her feet on the ground and her head out of the clouds, she told herself silently.

All Donovan Lancaster was offering her was a job, and a temporary one at that. Certainly nothing to get in a dither about, she reminded herself sternly. But she was in a dither, and as giddy as a young girl with her first boyfriend. Which was a fine state of affairs for a thirty-three-year-old woman, especially one who had always prided herself on her common sense. Much to her relief, the silent chastisement lent a measure of calm to her voice when she said, "That will be fine."

"Then six o'clock it is."

Nodding jerkily, he took a backward step. It was difficult, but he resisted the urge to check and see if he had two left feet. Shannon was so small and fragile that she made him feel about as graceful as a gorilla, and not a particularly intelligent one at that. He couldn't remember the last time he had been so flustered and unsure of himself—or if he ever had.

Shannon wasn't doing much better, but she at least remembered to ask him if he knew where her cousin lived. You're really losing it, Lancaster, Donovan thought sheepishly, a tinge of red darkening his broad cheekbones. "I'll get the address from Debra on my way out."

"Oh, of—of course," she stammered. "I'll see you tomorrow night, Donovan."

Oh, yes! His name sounded like melted honey on those lushly curved lips, he thought with a shiver, and he wondered if it would sound as sweet when she cried it out in passion. As she left him he watched the gentle sway of her pert, rounded little bottom in bemusement. He was going to find out before long, he promised himself. Either that, or he was going to start climbing walls in very short order.

Donovan parked his car in front of a modest yellow-and-white-trimmed tract home located in San Lorenzo Village, a small community sandwiched between San Leandro and Hayward. Cutting off the engine, he expelled a relieved breath as he once again peered at the metal numbers affixed to the side of the two-car garage. They matched the address he'd been given, which was a miracle, considering that most houses in this area looked very much alike.

For that matter, so did the streets, which were a veritable rabbit warren of twists and turns and cul-de-sacs. He should know, he decided with a wry quirk of his mouth. He had certainly been driving around long enough. Throwing open the car door, he slid his legs out and got to his feet. As he slammed the door shut again and began to walk toward the house, a dainty, red-haired vision in a snugly clinging lavender dress appeared on the front porch.

His footsteps faltered momentarily, and an odd sensation built around the region of his heart. "Hi," he murmured softly.

"Hi yourself."

Shannon took a moment to admire his tall figure, which was clad in gray slacks and a long-sleeved gold shirt that was casually unbuttoned at the throat. Her heart nearly pounding, she gestured for him to follow her inside the house with a flick of one slender, delicately formed hand. "Did you have any trouble finding us?"

He grimaced. "Since I'm nearly fifteen minutes late, and I'm generally a punctual man, you might say that. Debra's directions seemed as clear as springwater when I jotted them down, but I think she left out a couple of strategically necessary streets along the way."

Chuckling softly, Shannon gave him a look of heartfelt sympathy. "I should have warned you about her appalling sense of direction. She always talks about coming *up* to see me. I've tried to explain to her that the correct term is *down*, but Deb's reply is always the same."

In a credible imitation of her cousin's voice, she drawled, "I have to climb mountains to get there, don't I?" With a smirk, she added, "I wonder if she goes sideways to Reno?"

Donovan gave a shout of laughter, thoroughly entranced by Shannon's impish humor. He studied the teasing glint in her pretty green eyes and the lovely curve of her smile, and something inside him seemed to expand and reach toward her. He wanted to envelop himself in her inner beauty and bask in the warmth of her soul. He blinked in surprise, disconcerted by this sudden and unexpected leaning toward poetry.

He was also shaken by the strength of his desire to make a grab for her, and he gave a strained grimace that he hoped would pass for a smile. "Speaking of Debra, where is she?"

"If I know her, she's listening at a keyhole."

Right on cue, a grumbling voice sounded from the kitchen and a plump, indignant face framed by dark hair peered out at them. "Since my sliding door is open, I didn't need a keyhole to hear my name being taken in vain."

Pressing her hand against her chest, Shannon inquired innocently, "Would I do that?"

Debra lifted a single eyebrow and glanced at the smiling man taking up a good deal of her living room. "Ignore her," she advised. "She's just jealous because I'm prettier than she is. Like a cup of coffee before you go, Donovan?"

Although amused by the acerbic interplay between the two women, he was too eager to have Shannon to himself to countenance any further delay. "No thanks, Deb. I'm anxious to show Shannon around the grounds of the center before it gets too dark to see. We have floodlights for security reasons, but natural light gives a better impression."

Debra pursed her lips and angled her head to one side, her dark eyes gleaming shrewdly. "Pulling out all the stops to impress her, are you?"

"Through pure necessity," he replied with a grin. "I've been taking care of most of the cooking the past few days, and all my imagination runs to is soup. If I don't get someone in the kitchen who knows what they're doing, my staff is likely to round up the kids and form a lynch mob."

"Don't worry, your problems are over," Debra assured him. "Since she arrived Shannon's been fixing dinner for us, and she's an excellent cook. My husband went into ecstasies over her beef stew."

His eyes gleamed. "I'm partial to a good beef stew myself."

"But I have to warn you," she added, her eyes alight with mischief. "Shannon has a rather low threshold of boredom, and when she gets restless she paces. My carpets have barely held up under the strain."

He took note of the delicate flush that darkened Shannon's cheekbones at her cousin's teasing, and a twinkle lit his dark eyes as they slowly searched her features. His voice little more than a soft rasp pitched for her ears alone, he murmured, "I think I can keep her from being bored."

But the other woman's hearing was excellent, and Shannon's heart sank when she saw that Debra was practically quivering with curiosity. She recognized the look on her favorite relative's face, and she knew that in about ten seconds Deb was going to say something outrageous enough to make her wish she had never been born.

Shannon rushed to speak before the wickedly leering woman had a chance to open her mouth. "Well, I guess we'd better be on our way. Getting darker by the minute. See you later, Deb."

She darted past Donovan, and was through the door before he could do more than blink in surprise. He felt as though a whirling dervish had just passed by, and his side tingled from the light brush of her body against his. If such a brief, inconsequential contact could wreak this kind of havoc on his senses, he mused, how would it feel when he really touched her? Lord have mercy, the question boggled his mind!

With a shrug of his shoulders and a smile at Debra's amused countenance, he eagerly followed in Shannon's wake. His mouth went dry when his attention centered on the graceful sway of her hips as she crossed the lawn, and he wondered if she was as interested in him as he was in her. He didn't see how this strong an attraction could be one-sided, but stranger things had happened. With his luck, he would probably discover he was having a mid-life crisis!

It wouldn't surprise him, since his self-confidence seemed to have disappeared with Shannon's arrival. Women had never posed a problem for him, but they had never assumed much importance in his life, either. Since merely helping her into his car caused his hand to tremble, he had a hunch that she was going to prove to be quite a startling exception to that rule.

Giving himself a mental shake as he closed the door and circled the hood, he wondered if there really was such a thing as male menopause. If so, forty-two must be a prime age, since his hormones seemed determined to kick into overdrive. And he hadn't even known of Shannon's existence until yesterday, he realized in amazement. Why was he so preoccupied with her, and so eager to make a good impression? And why, he asked himself with a distinct twinge of anxiety, should her opinion of him matter so much?

As Donovan seated himself beside her, Shannon took note of the slight frown on his face. His distant manner increased her nervousness, and she wondered what she had said or done to bring about a return of the cold, taciturn stranger she had first met. Several miles passed as she contemplated the best way to break the uncomfortable silence that had fallen between them, and by then she was exasperated enough to opt for bluntness. "Have I done or said something to offend you?"

His brows lifted in a surprised arc as his head swiveled in her direction. "I beg your pardon?"

"Other than asking me to fasten my seat belt, you haven't said a single word to me since we got in this car, Mr. Lancaster."

His chest expanded on an indrawn breath, and his hands tightened on the steering wheel as he made a left onto the MacArthur Freeway. Once he had merged with the traffic in the center lane and was cruising at a reasonable speed, he again glanced over at Shannon. The strained expression on her face spoke volumes, and he cursed himself for his unintentional surliness. "I apologize for my rude behavior."

"It's me, isn't it?" she said. "When we were introduced, I got the impression you'd taken an instant dislike to me, and now I'm sure of it."

"That's nonsense. I don't dislike you, Shannon."

A muscle pulsed momentarily in his jaw, and he returned his eyes to the road as he attempted an explanation. "I haven't been alone with a woman in a while, and I guess I'm out of the habit of making small talk. To give it to you straight, I'm a little nervous, honey.''

Shannon sighed in relief and slumped against her seat. ''And here I've been worried all morning, wondering what in the world we were going to talk about.''

''I make you nervous?'' he questioned incredulously.

Her grin widened, and a sparkle of merriment danced in her eyes. ''To give it to you straight, you make me shake in my shoes.''

Donovan exited the freeway, his forehead pleated with perplexity. ''I don't see why.''

She studied the hands in her lap and loosened the death grip she had on her purse. ''You're obviously sophisticated and worldly. I'm not.''

They had just pulled up in front of the large wrought-iron gate that marked the entrance to Donovan's estate, and at her blunt statement he put the car in Park. For a moment he sat quietly, contemplating the view on the other side of his windshield, and then he looked at Shannon with a curiously intent expression in his eyes. ''Are you always this open with everyone?''

''I try to be,'' she remarked simply. ''I don't appreciate deceit in others, and I won't tolerate it in myself.''

He shook his head in bemusement. ''Then you're certainly different from most of the women I've known.''

A light ripple of laughter greeted his admission. ''Is that a nice way of telling me I'm an oddball?''

A spark of amusement flickered in his eyes. ''I'm saying I really like you, and that's not something I'm in the habit of admitting to females.''

''Women are just people, some likable and some not.''

''Most of those I've been involved with have fallen into the latter category.''

She slanted him a gamine's grin. ''Then why get involved with them?''

Donovan's brow rose in a wicked arc. "Can't you guess?"

He was deliberately trying to embarrass her. Although her cheeks colored, betraying her, Shannon played along with single-minded determination. "Shame on you, Mr. Lancaster."

When her eyes rose piously and her lips pursed in prim disapproval, he gave a shout of laughter and held out his hand. "Pax?" he asked contritely.

Shannon placed her fingers in his and tilted her head in inquiry. "Does this mean we're going to be friends?"

Donovan met her bright-eyed gaze head-on. "Is that what you want?" -

She quickly averted her head, afraid she might slip and tell him what she really wanted. Moistening her lips nervously, she whispered, "I could always use another friend."

It wasn't exactly the relationship he'd had in mind, but it would do for now. He looked down at the slender fingers he still held, glad his lowered lashes prevented her seeing the guilt he knew must be flaring to life in his eyes. "So could I, honey. So could I."

Three

Shannon's first sight of the three-story mansion located at the end of an oak-shaded drive proved to be a bit of a shock, especially when she compared it to the flame-ravaged hills they had passed to reach the estate. It was only then that she began to appreciate the devastating loss suffered by the community, in both historical and personal value, and to realize how close Donovan had come to losing his birthright.

Lancaster House was almost oppressively large, with eccentricities that were as charming as they were startling. Its gingerbread trim and crenellated attic turret were reminiscent of early Victorian architecture, an odd match for paned Cape Cod window embrasures and a wide white-columned porch and second-story balcony that owed their charm to the pre-Civil War South. The house stood in regal splendor, like a stately grande dame whose homely, irregular features had achieved grace and dignity with age.

Donovan turned into the graveled circular forecourt that fronted the huge building and parked the car. Releasing his seat belt, he leaned toward Shannon to share the view through the window on her side. Her soft hair brushed his cheek, and he closed his eyes on a surge of desire. He heard himself promising her friendship, and his guilt resurfaced with devastating force. She was a woman who hated deceit, he reminded himself, and yet he was lying to her by omission. As was to be expected, the thought didn't do much to ease his already nagging conscience.

Although achingly conscious of how close her cheek was to his mouth, he resisted the urge to place his lips against her warm flesh. "What do you think of the old barn?"

She turned rounded eyes in his direction. When she pursed her lips in a soundless whistle, Donovan stifled a groan and quickly assumed his former position. "Calling this place an old barn is like calling the *Mona Lisa* a pretty painting, Donovan."

"You didn't grow up here. When I was a young boy, I used to stand in the great room and yell just to hear my own voice echo back at me. It used to drive the servants crazy— not to mention my grandfather."

"Your grandfather raised you?"

Taking it for granted that he had been orphaned, she was shocked when he replied, "That was the agreement he made with my mother and father. They were to provide him with the heir he required, and he would make it possible for them to continue with their jet-setting life-style. He even wrote the agreement into his will—only now I'm the one who makes out the checks."

A hollow laugh erupted from his throat, and he shrugged his shoulders. "Although to say I was raised by the old man is something of an exaggeration, since he stuck me in military school back east as soon as I was old enough."

The loneliness in the admission caught at her heart. "How old were you?"

"Seven."

Shannon stared. "But you were hardly more than a baby!"

"At least then I had other kids to play with. When I returned during the summer and holiday seasons, this place seemed more like a tomb than ever. In retrospect, I guess I was glad to be home, but if old Lopez hadn't let me follow him around I would have been bored out of my skull."

"Lopez?" she questioned softly.

"Our head gardener. You'll meet him eventually."

"Didn't you have any friends of your own age visit you?"

His reply was blunt and to the point. "My grandfather didn't like children. In fact, he barely tolerated me, and only because I was a means of continuing the Lancaster line. Except in obliging him by taking part in an arranged marriage, my father was a big disappointment to him. The old man had alternately neglected and overindulged him, and he was determined not to make the same mistakes with me. But for all his diligence, he still failed to make me over into his sterling image."

From the little she had heard about his grandfather, Shannon only had one thing to say. "Thank heaven."

At her disparaging mutter, his eyes assumed a rather wicked gleam. "No, thanks to the public school system. As could have been predicted, I began to rebel against authority at about age fourteen. When I was expelled from school for the third time, Grandfather was forced to enroll me locally. Attending high school here was the best thing that could have happened to me."

But his levity failed to find a responsive chord in Shannon. Her continued dismay over the way he had been treated as a child was evident in the sympathetic shadowing of her expressive eyes. "Even so, if your grandfather was as hard-nosed as he sounds, it must have been a difficult adjustment for you."

"Since we didn't see much of each other, he and I rubbed along together pretty well after I returned home. His health had deteriorated drastically by then, and he rarely left his suite of rooms. Needless to say, my newfound freedom went to my head, and I ran wild. In school I specialized in girls and football instead of scholastics. I generally delighted in raising hell."

Shannon didn't miss the order in which he had placed his priorities, and a sudden burst of jealousy had her reeling in shock. Her emotional reaction was absurd, to say the least. Of course he had taken a healthy interest in girls when he was growing up, she told herself silently. She had been just as interested in boys, for pity's sake. Just because she now lagged rather drastically behind him in experience and sophistication, that was no reason for her to develop some kind of idiotic complex at this stage in her life.

Somewhat hurriedly, she attempted to shake off her self-consciousness with a smile. When her lips failed to respond as fulsomely as she wished, she shifted uneasily in the confines of the bucket seat. His attention caught by her restless movements, Donovan suggested they start their tour. "The entire property runs to ten acres, so we'd better stick to the cleared paths closest to the shelter for now. If you'd like, I'll give you an extended tour at a later date."

He didn't wait for her to reply. Throwing open his door, he emerged in a single fluid movement. A shiver coursed through Shannon's slender frame as she watched him circle the hood, his clothing unable to disguise the powerful grace of his muscular frame. As he drew close enough to open the door for her, her mouth went dry and her palms grew moist.

When she rose to stand beside him, their bodies briefly brushed against each other. Shannon bit back a gasp, tingling from the innocent contact. But her reaction to him was not at all innocent, and she rushed into speech to try to control the carnal direction of her thoughts. "I gather from the way Tricia talked that you and her brother have been friends for years. Did the two of you meet in high school?''

He shook his head. "Drew is quite a few years my junior. He had gotten his pant leg caught in the chain of his bike, and I stopped to untangle him."

Shannon gave him a look of approval. "I have a couple of teenage nephews, and on the whole they're pretty terrific guys. But if my memory serves me correctly, they view grade school kids with extreme disdain. I doubt if either of them would have paid much attention to Drew's predicament, let alone stopped to help."

With a casual shrug, he began to envision the scene from his past. A tiny curve indented one corner of his mouth as they rounded the side of the house and headed toward a stand of trees along the rear of the property. "Drew was a little difficult to ignore. He was sprawled in the middle of a crosswalk, screaming bloody murder at the top of his lungs."

Donovan chuckled at the memory and shook his head. "Afterward, I couldn't get rid of the persistent little brat, but he kind of grew on me. And his folks trusted me to look out for him, which meant a lot to me."

Shannon's attention was caught by the gentle note that had entered his voice upon mention of the elder Sinclairs. With a smile, she said, "They were obviously good judges of character."

"In those days you couldn't tell much about my character by the way I dressed and acted, that was for sure. By my sophomore year I'd developed some pretty rough edges, and I was carrying a chip on my shoulder heavier than the national debt. I was also starting to get into trouble, and not just in school. Luckily for me, the Sinclairs saw through my arrogant, smart-mouthed facade from the beginning. They soon set me straight."

Pausing beside a clump of manzanita, he braced his foot on a sturdy red root and sighed. "They really cared, you know? For the first time I saw what a real home could be like, and they made me feel like part of their family.''

Returning his foot to the ground, he directed his gaze toward a line of cypress trees standing sentinel on the horizon. She saw his throat convulse briefly as he swallowed, and her own throat tightened with emotion at the vulnerable look in his eyes. ''The love and guidance they gave me made all the difference in my life.''

Her eyes widened in sudden comprehension. ''That's why you opened this shelter, isn't it? So you could make a difference for a lot of other kids.''

''You're partially correct, but not entirely.'' He hesitated briefly and gestured her toward a stone bench beside the path. Once they were seated, he leaned forward, bracing his elbows on his knees as he stared down at his linked fingers. ''A stint in Vietnam was the real turning point in my life, Shannon.''

Donovan's features tightened into an unrevealing mask, but the slight tremor in his hands belied his surface calm. He had made it out of Vietnam alive and relatively unscathed, he thought bitterly, except in spirit. But the war that wasn't had taken its toll, destroying the boy he had been and replacing him with a man who desperately needed to find some meaning to life. A man who felt there had to be a reason for his survival. One who suffered a deep-rooted guilt for having escaped that hellhole when so many of his comrades hadn't been so fortunate.

Glancing at the woman beside him, he said, ''I was given a firsthand view of the atrocities men can inflict on one another, and I hated what the war was forcing me to become.''

His voice thick with disgust, he shook his head and gazed blindly down at the ground. ''I found myself killing out of an animal instinct for survival, not because of any idealistic beliefs. If I wanted to preserve my sanity, I had to find a reason to justify my presence there. Do you understand, Shannon?''

Her eyes stung as she nodded, but she was unable to force a single syllable past her constricted throat. She could only try to imagine what it must have been like for a sensitive, sheltered young man to be thrust into the nightmare that had been Vietnam, and she knew her imagination must fall far short of reality. She wanted to say something—anything— to wipe away the horrible memories she could glimpse in Donovan's eyes, but all she could do was listen.

''We couldn't do anything to stop the bloodshed,'' he continued harshly, ''so some of my friends and I decided to do what we could to help the youngest casualties of war. There were so many sick, hungry, homeless kids wandering the streets of Saigon, begging or stealing or selling their bodies to survive. With the financial aid we received from the U.S., we set up several crisis centers to provide some of them with the necessities to sustain life.''

Donovan's story drew to a close. As she studied his with-drawn features, Shannon doubted if he was even aware of her presence. He was in another time and place, and she couldn't follow him there. She ached to call him back to her, to ease the torment she saw in his eyes, but she didn't know how. When the silence between them threatened to become awkward, she whispered, ''It must have been difficult for you to leave the children behind when you were sent home.''

''It was, until I returned and discovered kids who were victims of another kind of injustice,'' he remarked curtly. ''Those who sought escape from abusive situations. Those who had fallen through the cracks in a complex social structure. The misfits who soon discovered that the streets were a war zone they hadn't expected to find. Like the rag-ged urchins in Vietnam, they needed help to survive. Thanks to my inheritance from my grandfather, my staff and I do what we can. It's never enough, but it's better than noth-ing.''

Shannon inhaled a reviving breath, but had to clear her throat before she could speak. "I'm certain your grandfather would have been proud of you, Donovan."

To her consternation, a loud bark of laughter greeted her words. "The old man would roll over in his grave if he knew what I'd done with my inheritance."

Shannon gaped at him. "Surely not!"

His lips twitched with amusement. "I'm afraid so."

"Then he didn't deserve a grandson like you," she snapped indignantly. "Anyone with an ounce of compassion would admire the work you do."

Donovan took note of her extreme indignation without surprise, since he had already guessed at the tender, nurturing personality she possessed. But it seemed that gentle nature of hers was accompanied by a fiercely protective streak, and having all that stalwart emotion directed toward him did odd things to his heart rate. Suddenly the urge to touch her returned with such force that he was shocked by the extent of his need.

Unable to stop himself, he lifted his hand and gently brushed his knuckle along the slender column of her neck. A sweetly clinging tendril immediately wrapped itself around his forefinger, and he smiled indulgently. "We're little more than strangers. You're very quick to champion someone you barely know."

Even though her grin held an endearing impishness, her response was certain and straightforward. "You don't seem like a stranger to me, Donovan."

His gaze lingered in the forested depths of her eyes for the space of a heartbeat, as he became aware of a similar sense of familiarity. His voice a little on the shaky side, he said, "I know what you mean. You do strange things to my psyche, woman."

Shannon's entire body quivered with nerves as she inwardly acknowledged her own vulnerability to the intriguing, intensely virile man at her side. His golden eyes had a way of short-circuiting her thoughts whenever he looked at her, but she wasn't quite certain she could trust the way she was feeling toward him. She studied the forceful, decisive angle of his jawline, and her attention automatically drifted toward the softer, more sensual curve of his mouth.

She wanted to kiss him so badly she could taste it!

Immediately panicked at the realization, she jumped up and glanced down at him nervously. "It's a-almost dark, and I'm a-anxious to see the inside of Lancaster House," she stammered. "Will we have time for a look before dinner?"

"We'll make time for the essentials." He got to his feet, grasped her arm and guided her in a new direction. "Come on. I'll show you a shortcut."

The next hour was taken up with meeting a confusing array of the shelter's residents, both young and not so young, negotiating an endless number of corridors and hallways, and admiring the imposing architecture of bygone days. Gilded cornices, cathedral ceilings, original hardwood floors that gleamed with a rich patina, all blended together to leave Shannon nearly speechless with awe. Lancaster House was so big it was hard on the feet. By the time Donovan glanced at his watch and suggested they head back to the car, she was calculating the miles she had walked with an inward groan of protest.

Descending a curved flight of stairs from the second story, she ran her hand caressingly along the intricately carved banister railing. She had never seen anything to equal its elegance, unless she counted a remembered scene from the movie *Gone with the Wind*. A sudden image leaped into her mind, one that knocked the breath right out of her. She saw Donovan carrying her up this staircase in his strong arms, the way Rhett had Scarlett. Just the thought of where those two had been headed was enough to leave her tingling from head to toe.

Rather later than planned, they drove away from the shelter to a chorus of goodbyes. Shannon turned toward Donovan with a pleased grin. "Your staff made me feel right at home, and young Trina's a darling, isn't she?"

At her reference to one of his permanent boarders, he nodded in agreement. "She's anxious to please. If you like, I'll assign her to kitchen duty while you're working here."

"Will she mind?" Picturing the girl's sweet face and remembering how anxious she had seemed when they were introduced, Shannon frowned uncertainly. "Helping me prepare meals in that monstrous kitchen won't be a picnic. I don't want her to feel pressured, Donovan."

"Don't worry," he replied with a laugh. "While Sam was showing you the last dormitory room, Trina assaulted me in the hall. She practically begged to be your assistant while you're working here. I figure she liked you enough to risk dishpan hands.

"And what about you?" he asked as he began to brake. The car's headlights illuminated the wrought-iron gates in front of them, but his attention was centered on her shadowed profile. "Do you think you'll like living here?"

"Living here?"

He heard the surprised note in her voice as the car drew to a halt, and he frowned as he pressed the button on the dash that activated the automatic gate mechanism. "You did realize that this would be a live-in position, didn't you? The kitchen is run in split shifts, which doesn't allow for anything else."

"But I just assumed, since I'm only going to be working there for about two weeks..."

"You'll have a suite of rooms off the kitchen with a private bath, so you won't lack for privacy." His eyes narrowing as he studied her hesitant expression, he added, "If you're worried about your safety, most of my security staff are housed in the same wing."

The thought had never entered her head, and she was quick to tell him so. Immediately his frown deepened, his features conveying a warning. "Don't ever make the mistake of becoming too complacent about your safety while you're here, Shannon. Never walk the far grounds unless accompanied by a male staff member, and make certain you lock the door of your quarters both night and day as a precaution against theft. The kids we house are a pretty mixed bag, and most are no angels."

"I realize that."

"Maybe technically you do, but that basic understanding won't give you the whole picture of what you'll be dealing with on a day-to-day basis. We're able to straighten out some of the kids, but most are beyond our help. They have a firsthand knowledge of the seamier side of humanity, with an emphasis on drugs, prostitution and other crimes that would make those carrot curls of yours stand on end."

Resisting the urge to reprimand him for his unflattering reference to her hair color, she asked, "Do you ever turn kids away?"

"Only if we're full up, or if they've already blotted their copybook with us," he replied. "We try to keep troublemakers at a minimum, but we don't ask for personal references when they come to us, Shannon. A few of our regulars, like Sam and Trina, are seriously attempting to better themselves. Unfortunately, they're outnumbered ten to one by hard-core transients, those who've been on the streets too long."

She gazed at him curiously. "Does the length of time they've been on the streets make that much difference in their behavior, Donovan?"

He responded to her question with a question of his own, one that was more graphic than she would have liked. "If a good-natured puppy is starved and brutalized during its formative months of growth, what will you end up with, honey?"

She winced visibly. "I get the picture."

His face lost all expression, but his body tensed betrayingly. "Now that I've thoroughly alarmed you, do you think you can handle the job? Cooking for that mob back there won't be easy, even with split shifts and what assistance I can provide for you. I wouldn't want to overtax your strength, especially when you're probably still not a hundred percent fit after your illness."

"But I am." She brushed aside his concern with an impatient wave of her small hand. "And compared to my nursing duties, working at Lancaster House will be a piece of cake."

Donovan didn't believe that for a moment, but the relief he felt at her decision was almost tangible. "Then the position is yours, Ms. Dalton. I'll come by for you in the morning and help you get moved."

Her eyes sparkled, and she formed her fingers into a military salute. "Yes, sir!"

Donovan burst out laughing at her unexpected response, and a smile lingered on his mouth as he drove away from the estate. He was enchanted by the woman at his side. Her multifaceted personality was as sparkling and full of brilliance as the most beautiful crystal-clear diamond. She was beautifully, naturally sensuous, a delightful bundle of femininity who had broken through his self-imposed isolation with startling ease.

She wasn't cold and self-seeking, like most of the women he had known over the years, nor was she someone who would take intimacy lightly. She was a warm, kindhearted female with a great deal of empathy for others. Those were traits that left her damnably in danger of being hurt by him. He didn't appreciate being thwarted by his own instincts, but his urge to protect her seemed to be as strong as his desire to get her into his bed.

As they were shown to their seats at one of his favorite restaurants, Donovan watched as Shannon engaged their hostess in conversation. Her manner was relaxed and openly friendly, and he suddenly felt ashamed of the salaciousness of the thoughts he had initially had about her. If she had been able to read his mind at the time, she probably would have slapped him. No, he mused with inward amusement, she would most likely have doubled up her small fist and slugged him square in his arrogant nose!

And he would have deserved it, he decided with disgusted certainty. He hadn't realized how jaded and cynical his attitude toward the fairer sex had become, or how predictable. However, even a blind idiot like him could see that Shannon was different, and he was determined to gain her respect. She wanted friendship, and he was going to do his best to give it to her. While she worked for him, he was going to keep his libido in line, he told himself sternly, or die trying.

With that decision firmly implanted in his head, he seated her and then himself and glanced across the table with a casual smile. "If you don't like Italian food, they serve a mean steak here."

"I adore pasta, but I'm probably too excited to do justice to a meal. I'm looking forward to working for you, Donovan."

"And you won't mind living at the shelter?"

"Quite the contrary. I'm going to enjoy my new surroundings immensely."

"You really were impressed by the old place, weren't you?"

"Impressed isn't quite the word I would choose." She peered at him over the menu she had just been handed. "Compared to the modest bungalow in L.A. where I grew up, entering Lancaster House was like stepping into another world of ageless grace and timeless beauty."

Donovan gave a snort of derision, his expression sardonic. "Now that you mention it, growing up there was a little like falling down the rabbit hole. But, like Alice, I never quite fit into Wonderland.''

She laughed lightly. "I don't think I would have, either. At heart I'm a simple, no-frills kind of person.''

It was odd, but Donovan believed her implicitly. When he considered how accustomed he had become to selfish, grasping women—like his own mother—he couldn't help but be shocked by his reaction to Shannon. There was a sweet innocence about her, he decided thoughtfully, a lack of pretense and a goodness of heart that he trusted instinctively. The realization saddened him.

It also brought pain in its wake, because a long time ago there might have been a chance for them. A chance to share a home and children, and to live a normal existence. But that had been before Vietnam fashioned him into the man he was today. The shelter and the kids he worked with there had become his saving grace, but he would be the first to admit that his work didn't make for an easy life. It would be unfair to expect a woman to share his responsibilities, especially someone as gentle and sensitive as the one seated across from him.

"I hate it when you do that.''

He was absentmindedly tracing the pattern on the white linen tablecloth when she spoke, and his head jerked upward in surprise. "When I do what?''

She scrunched her face into a ferocious scowl, then grinned. "You can be very intimidating, Mr. Lancaster.''

"You don't seem cowed, Ms. Dalton.'' He angled his head to one side, his dark eyes warm with approval. "But that's probably because you know that one of your smiles would earn you an easy victory in most confrontations.''

Shannon thought of all the children she and her team had struggled futilely to save. "I wish that were true, but sometimes the odds are stacked too heavily against any possibility of victory, Donovan.''

Something inside him twisted in sympathy at the tremor of pain he heard in her voice. He suddenly wished he could reach into her mind and excise that unpleasant memory, to keep her from ever being hurt again. Then he wondered if he would be able to protect her from him, and quickly thrust the thought from his mind.

"That's the way growing up was for me," he finally said. "A lesson in futility, with me struggling to live up to my grandfather's exacting standards. Although I guess I shouldn't have tried. His ideas weren't structured to deal with the everyday world."

"But you've certainly learned to deal with that world now, Donovan."

His mouth curved cynically. "It was about time one of the Lancasters paid his dues."

Shannon saw his fingers clench around the stem of his water glass, and she wasn't at all surprised by the reproachful tone in his voice. This man carried so many scars, she thought, and from wounds that should never have been inflicted. Yet he had countered adversity with dignity and courage. He, of all people, shouldn't have to suffer from a guilty conscience, she decided with a fierce surge of protectiveness, just because he'd been born with a surfeit of worldly goods.

A man like this one didn't ask for whom the bell tolls, she thought whimsically. From what she had seen, he was uniquely attuned to its resonance, an outwardly brusque individual whose inflexible facade concealed a strong sense of duty and a remarkable degree of compassion and understanding. It was just a shame that the rigid, indomitable old tyrant who had raised him hadn't valued those characteristics.

Instead, that obviously shallow, self-righteous individual had attempted to destroy the very qualities in his grandson of which he should have been most proud. Studying the stubborn cast of Donovan's features with an inward smile, she decided it was little wonder that the elder Lancaster had failed. It was impossible not to sense the intrinsic goodness in the proud man the neglected boy had grown into, and she suddenly felt a strong urge to make up for all the affection he had never received in his childhood.

What would it be like, she wondered breathlessly, to press her head against his chest and hold him close? She could almost hear the steady beating of his heart against her ear, testifying to a life force that could submerge her within itself only too easily. When she considered her own strength of will, the pleasure she felt at the fanciful notion both dismayed and intrigued her.

Shannon had always valued her independence. Even as a child in a crowded household, she had zealously maintained her autonomy. Yet as she clasped her hands tightly together in her lap, she let herself contemplate what it might be like to share herself with a man like Donovan Lancaster. How would it feel to experience the kind of devoted relationship her own parents still enjoyed after nearly forty years of marriage? To have a man love her enough to take the good with the bad, the joy with the sorrow?

You thought you'd found that man once, an inner voice reminded her, *and look how wrong you were.* The warning served to shore up her defenses, much to her relief. She was really going to have to keep better control over her imagination, she decided grimly, or she was going to talk herself into trouble with a capital *T.* Or Donovan with a capital *D,* she thought, suppressing a hysterical desire to giggle.

Anyway, all this soul-searching was a ridiculous waste of time. She had already relegated Donovan to the status of friend, and that was right where she was going to keep him. The distaste she felt at the thought infuriated her. Was she losing her mind? she asked herself incredulously. She had taken a shot at romance, and emerged from the relationship sadder but wiser. Surely she had learned that painful lesson too well to put herself through the emotional wringer again?

Since the end of her engagement, she had been careful to keep her relationships with the opposite sex casual and uninvolved. So why, she wondered with a twinge of fear, was she reacting to this man so differently? What was it about him that made her crave something more than she already had? Until recently, she had been fairly contented with her life, and she would be again if she had any say in the matter.

Reassured by her thoughts, Shannon regained Donovan's attention with a light, if slightly tremulous, trill of laughter. "Have I put you to sleep?"

His expression sheepish, he said, "You're probably wishing you had."

She arched her brow curiously, and he admitted, "I haven't run off at the mouth like this since I was a kid. Normally I'm a rather dour character, without much to say for myself."

Pleasure softened her features. "I'm glad you feel you can talk to me."

Their gazes collided as she spoke, and a quivering awareness erupted between them. Donovan felt the breath become suspended in his lungs, while Shannon trembled from the unspoken communication passing between them. She sensed a crumbling of old inhibitions, while he experienced a wealth of unfamiliar emotions.

Donovan looked away first, immensely relieved to see a waiter approaching the table. God alone knew how badly he needed a distraction at that moment. "Have you decided what to order?"

Shannon nodded, and she told him her preference in a calm voice, though her thoughts were in turmoil. Since meeting Donovan, she had run the gamut of emotional reactions: irritation, bewilderment, admiration and tenderness. Not to mention the physical chemistry between them, which was strong enough to make her question her usual policy of noninvolvement.

She was already alarmingly vulnerable to his appeal, and if she had any sense at all she would leave and push him from her mind while she had the chance. That it might already be too late for such an evasive maneuver was a thought that struck at the core of her being, a supposition that she denied with every ounce of rationality she possessed.

Yet all of a sudden she found it difficult to catch her breath, as though all the oxygen had just been removed from a twilight zone of her own making. She was entering an unfamiliar realm, she realized, one in which she felt trapped by a sense of inevitability, a victim of a capricious—and not entirely trustworthy—fate.

Four

Donovan walked slowly down the dirt path that led from his cottage to Lancaster House, his head bent as he contemplated the happenings of the past five days. Shannon had settled into her routine with an ease that had astounded him. Not for a moment had she seemed uptight or uncomfortable in her new surroundings, as most of his employees were in the beginning. He had expected her to be nervous, even frightened, around some of their more reprehensible residents, but she'd never once let a scruffy appearance or a foul mouth intimidate her.

Since she had taken over in the kitchen, it had become the heart of the shelter. By her second day at work, it had become impossible to enter her domain without tripping over one person or another, whether staff or residents. Shannon had a knack for listening, and a genuine interest in people—two qualities that helped her assimilate easily with their enclosed society. She was also quite capable of standing up for herself.

And she did so without ever having to raise her voice. Whenever she was goaded by one of their more obnoxious boarders, she had a way of silencing the heckler with a calm, straightforward look that spoke volumes. As far as he'd been able to tell, few had tried putting her down a second time. She also never seemed to hold a grudge, and was always quick to put an unpleasant incident behind her. Indeed, her sunny, vibrant personality seemed to act like a magnet, drawing everyone she came into contact with into her orbit. He was certainly no exception.

He had spent every free moment glued to her side, either helping her in the kitchen or taking her out in the evenings to show her the sights. Oh, he had given both herself and himself a couple of very logical reasons to account for his attentiveness, he recalled wryly. Once he had spouted some drivel about helping her establish an easy routine in the kitchen, so that she wouldn't overtax her strength and become ill again. And on another occasion he had offered to show her some of the tourist attractions the Bay Area had to offer, but of course that had been so that she wouldn't miss anything by helping him out.

Such marked thoughtfulness and consideration, he mused derisively. In actual fact his motives were far from selfless where she was concerned. The simple truth was, he needed to be with her, needed the warmth of her smile, the sound of her laughter, the soft, husky tone of her voice. She made him feel complete. His craving for her time and attention went beyond anything he had ever experienced before. Certainly beyond friendship. He had spent many restless hours pacing the floors of his cottage, wondering just what the hell he thought he was doing.

She was getting to him as no other woman ever had, and it wasn't just her sweet, silky body he wanted to possess. He had never wanted a woman in quite this way before, the knowledge of her heart and mind as important to him as his sexual needs. What was worse, he didn't know what to do about it. She was the marrying kind, and he was not. He couldn't bear the thought of her leaving, yet neither could he feel right about asking her to stay.

Although she wasn't due to report back to work until January, he didn't think it would be fair to lead her on in a relationship that at best could only be temporary. Nor would it be fair to let her become too attached to the kids at the shelter, which she was already in danger of doing. Donovan knew only too well what it was like to lose a promising child to the streets, and he never wanted Shannon to experience the guilt and sense of helplessness that resulted from such a failure. Nursing was a difficult and demanding profession, but taking temperatures and wiping runny noses in some doctor's office couldn't possibly come close to the kind of debilitating reality she would encounter if she remained here.

Right now this place was a novelty, but it would lose its appeal after a few doses of disillusionment. He knew it, and yet it wasn't something he found easy to accept. His growing need for her was beginning to overshadow his good sense. But no matter how many times he told himself that he was thinking like a selfish bastard, he was tempted to demand more from her than she should be asked to give.

The trouble was, she made him dream foolish and impossible dreams. He wanted more than a few nights in her arms, and that knowledge scared the living daylights out of him. Yet acknowledging the full extent of his vulnerability where she was concerned didn't lessen his desire for her. Nor did it prevent him from trying to convince himself that an affair, however brief, might be beneficial to them both.

Raising his head, he glanced over the treetops at the setting sun, with a feeling of futility. Another day almost over, and he was no closer to making a decision regarding Shannon than he had been the day before. His judgment was flawed by need, and he didn't trust himself where she was concerned. If they became lovers, it wouldn't make their parting any less inevitable. Eventually she would return to the life she knew, the life that was right for her. When that day came, would either of them be able to face the future without bitterness and regret? Was a brief period of pleasure worth a lifetime of pain?

He wasn't able to answer those questions, and until he could he knew he should distance himself from her. But knowing what he should do and doing it were two very different propositions. His conscience might be urging caution, he thought sardonically, but his flesh was damnably weak. For once he wanted to live for the moment and say to hell with the consequences.

All his senses were attuned to her, and every particle of his being told him she would come to him willingly. That certainty had little to do with male conceit, and a great deal to do with a pair of expressive eyes. At times he had seen his own desire mirrored in their depths, and with it a tenderness that caught at his heart.

Shannon would give herself with the same generosity of spirit that was so intrinsic to her nature, and that thought alone was enough to erode his powers of resistance. Dear Lord, how badly he wished he could take her somewhere safe! A soft, gentle place for lovers, where nothing and no one could come between them.

Donovan kicked viciously at a rock in his path and watched it sail into the air and disappear into a clump of manzanita. He was like that sturdy, green-leaved bush, he decided with a cynical twist of his lips—too damn stubborn and unyielding to change. He wouldn't be easily uprooted from this place; nor would it be possible to have this place uprooted from him.

Shoving his hands into the pockets of his jeans, he shook his head despondently. There was no way out for him, and the sooner he accepted that, the better it would be, for both him and Shannon. Slowly he forced himself to continue walking toward the tall building that was just visible through the trees, and the woman whose presence made it seem, for the first time in his memory, like a real home.

The following day heralded the weekend, and Saturday night Donovan took Shannon to see a delightful musical comedy at the Curren Theater in San Francisco. Afterward they drove to Fisherman's Wharf and enjoyed a late supper by candlelight. The restaurant smelled deliciously of seafood and spice-scented candles, and their linen-draped table was placed in front of a glass wall that overlooked the ocean.

A black-velvet sky was adorned with a thousand twinkling stars, and there was a fat yellow moon that served as a beacon for the rolling, wind-tossed surf. It was a magical evening, one of the most enjoyable Shannon had ever spent, and she didn't want it to end. All of her outings with Donovan had been delightful, but tonight seemed somehow magical. She felt special...almost cherished...in the company of this man.

Glancing shyly up at him as he unlocked the passenger door of his car, she said, "I've had a wonderful time, Donovan. I wish tonight could last forever."

He gazed into the sparkling depths of her eyes, and his good intentions galloped away with his heartbeat. "How about a walk on the beach before we head back?"

The air was warm—it was a perfect Indian-summer day—and she didn't hesitate to accept. "That sounds like a marvelous idea."

Marvelous, but not wise, Donovan thought as he helped her into the car and walked around to the driver's side. But he deliberately wiped his mind free of doubts, determined to steal another hour with her. It didn't take long for them to arrive at their destination, a lovely section of coastline he had once visited with Drew and Maria. There was a steep descent to the beach to be negotiated, but he had the feeling that Shannon would find the walk well worth the effort.

A short distance from the cliff's edge, a stand of towering rocks jutted up from the sandy soil, providing a secluded haven for those who sought privacy from the highway above. Since theirs was the only vehicle parked on the verge of the road near the entrance to the cove, privacy was just what they were going to get. A little kick of excitement accelerated his pulse at the thought.

There was a lightweight polyester car cover in the trunk that would serve them well as a makeshift beach blanket. As Shannon took advantage of his absence to remove her nylons and shoes, he withdrew the bulky material from the trunk with a boyish anticipation he found slightly embarrassing. When she joined him, he tore off his own footwear and eagerly reached for her hand to guide her down the path toward the beach.

"Oh, Donovan, this is lovely," she murmured as they reached their destination.

The warm, lambent glow in his eyes rivaled the sultry moon for brilliance, and Shannon trembled slightly as she glanced up at him. The huge, shadowed gray rocks behind them formed a welcome windbreak, and also gave an illusion of isolation from the outside world. Together, they spread the ground cover upon a smooth patch of sand, and then they turned as one and raced toward the welcoming surf.

"Donovan—wait!"

Shannon grabbed at a brawny arm as they reached the damp sand left by the outgoing tide. He had removed his jacket and tie along with his shoes and socks, but there was still a pair of expensive-looking black slacks to contend with. She wanted to wade in the surf like a water sprite, and she wanted him to join her at her play. "You'd better roll up your pants before you get them all wet."

Instantly he reached for his belt, a wicked grin curving his mouth. He hooked his thumbs over the edge, and his fingers brushed the slim silver buckle. The devilish gleam in his eyes belied the innocent inflection in his voice. "Why don't we strip down and go skinny-dipping?"

His white dress shirt was unbuttoned halfway down his broad chest, and the full sleeves were billowing in the balmy breeze. Shannon was entranced by the picture he made, and her thoughts were dreamy as she studied his wide-legged stance. He looked as rakishly irresistible as a pirate straight out of a romance novel, and just as sexy.

But suddenly his suggestion registered in her fantasy-drugged mind, and the breath left her body in a startled rush. She had been raised by two wonderful but very conventional parents. While not exactly old-fashioned, they had instilled strong moral values in their offspring. Good girls did not go skinny-dipping when accompanied by gorgeous men with golden come-hither eyes. Yet right now she was tempted to lower the spaghetti straps from her shoulders and shimmy out of her wispy chiffon gown without her usual self-conscious inhibitions.

Donovan reacted instantly to the brief flicker of hesitation in her eyes, the beating of his pulse beginning to rival the roaring thunder of the sea. Just as swiftly, he felt his body tightening with need. Without conscious volition, he moved closer to her, his breathing as unsteady as his heartbeat. His voice was a husky rasp of sound, a whisper of temptation in the night. "Shannon?"

Her name was followed by an audible breath that farther widened the open vee of his shirt. Her gaze fell on a tantalizing glimpse of dark golden body hair. It was a curly tangle that looked as soft as the hair on his head, and she ached to reach out and touch him there. Maybe it was the very intensity of her emotions that pulled her back from the brink, because suddenly she was evading his outstretched hand.

With an unsteady trill of laughter, she began to run along the shore, her dancing feet playing tag with the foamy surf. Breathing heavily, Donovan closed his eyes against the sight of her loveliness, but could do nothing to curtail his thoughts. In that dove gray piece of witchery she wore, she was the embodiment of all his dreams, a gorgeous nymph bathed in moonlight mist. He could hear her calling to him, beckoning him to join her in paying homage to nature's incredible display of power and beauty.

Years of constraint and self-control fell away from him in an instant, and with a joyous yell he ran after her, his feet flying over the sand. He didn't worry about wet hems or anything else as he joined her, and they cavorted together like children in a paradise of their own making. But in some ways they were unlike children, for every teasing touch increased their growing awareness of each other. Every breathless gasp spun them into a vortex of excitement, and every look branded their senses with desire.

What happened next was as inevitable as tomorrow, and as undeniable as yesterday. Shannon's foot caught on a tangled mass of seaweed, and Donovan caught her before she could fall. Lifting her up with a shout of triumph, he began whirling her around and around in a dizzying circle. With a lighthearted giggle, she wrapped her arms around his neck and felt the world fall away as she gazed into his eyes.

His feet stilled abruptly, and his chest rose and fell on a ragged sigh. Their laughter was borne away on a sea-scented breath of wind, and the silence that crept between them was rife with a sexual tension they could no longer pretend didn't exist. Feeling like a man caught up in a fantasy, he carried her across the sand. Kneeling on their makeshift blanket, he lowered his sweet burden with a gentleness and a tender concern that caused her heart to flood with warmth.

Shannon caught her breath at the look of near reverence that had softened his strong features, and suddenly all the doubts and fears of the past week dissolved into nothingness. For the first time since meeting him, she acknowledged her true feelings for this dark-eyed, enigmatic man. He was already a part of her, and she accepted the inevitability of this moment without question.

"Donovan," she whispered achingly.

His responsive gasp was muffled against her soft mouth as his tongue licked at her lips as though he were starved for the taste and texture of her flesh. He drank of her sweet moistness with the eagerness of a man dying of thirst, and steadied his shaking hands against the firm breasts that arched into his cupping palms.

Until he heard the sliding rasp of a zipper, he wasn't even aware that his fingers had searched out the fastening at the back of her gown. His shirt was lying in the sand beside them, and he couldn't remember which of them had removed it. He reclined beside her, with no memory of having lowered himself to the ground. All he could think of was the woman he held against him in the moonlight. Her name was an endless, echoing litany in his heart and his passion-dazed mind.

While he slipped the slim straps of her dress off her satin-soft shoulders, his mouth sought to imprint itself on every inch of her face. His seeking lips pressed against every shadowed dip and every delicate curve, finally sliding over her rounded chin to explore the pulsing hollow of her throat. Her anguished moan vibrated against the tip of his tongue as he tasted her there, and he smiled his pleasure at the sound of her passion.

Shannon wore no bra, and his eyes delighted in the delicious bounty his hands had uncovered. The moon dappled her creamy flesh with a pearlescent glow, and provided a perfect backdrop for dusky rose nipples that proudly attested to her state of arousal. "You are perfection itself," he said huskily.

"I'm not too small?"

He heard the self-consciousness in her voice with surprise, and the shyness with understanding. He lifted his head and glanced down at her. His expression was tender as he gently cupped his palm over one firmly resilient mound. "You fit into my hand as though you were made for me."

Shannon's fingers slid over his naked shoulders in a slow caress that made him shiver, and she clutched at his muscular biceps as she drew him down to her. Her lips traced the strong, tense line of his jaw until she reached his ear. She paused at the entrance to that small orifice and murmured, "You make me feel as if I were made for you, Donovan."

The hot, gliding tip of her tongue followed her words, and with a tortured cry he rolled on top of her. His eyes were wild with a passion greater than anything he had ever hoped to find. As he braced his weight on his forearms and cradled her head between his hands, his drumming heart matched the powerful cadence of hers. "You are a beautiful and desirable woman, but so fragile and delicate I'm almost afraid to touch you. Am I too heavy for you?"

"Oh, no, you feel wonderful...." Her eyes eloquent with emotion, she clutched at his forearms to keep him from withdrawing. "Kiss me again. Please . . . kiss me."

Their open mouths met and dueled and mated together, while his searching hips found the soft cradle of her femininity with a sensation of homecoming. Shannon slid her hands over his furry chest and down his lean sides, and wanted to scream in frustration when her arms failed to completely surround his broad back.

A small sound of dissatisfaction did escape her throat, and she shifted restlessly beneath him. She wanted to absorb his body with her own, and bind him to her for an eternity. She wanted them to meld into one being, with no beginning and no end for either of them. She wanted more than she had ever wanted from any man—even the one she had nearly married.

Donovan moaned as he felt her move beneath him. He was nearly at the end of his endurance, his thickly engorged manhood pressing painfully against his slacks. But it was a pain he welcomed, one that suddenly brought the outside world back into focus. He couldn't take her here, he realized in anguish, on a public beach where anyone might come along. He couldn't take her at all, not without hating himself even more than he did already.

With a choked cry, he rolled to one side, and jackknifed into a sitting position beside her. He drew his legs up and circled them with his arms, then lowered his forehead to his knees while he struggled to calm himself. His gut convulsed in agonizing cramps, but his mind was trying to grapple with what he had almost let happen. Gritting his teeth, he muttered, "For the love of heaven, no more!"

Shannon stared at his broad back, her flushed cheeks slowly draining of color. "Donovan, I—"

"Please . . . fix your gown, honey. I don't want to touch you again."

The cruel admission devastated her, but she managed to do as he asked. She lifted the bodice of her dress until it covered her breasts, while a swift, burning resentment overpowered the pain of his rejection. "I never asked you to start."

"Or to stop," he muttered gratingly.

Shannon cried out at the unfairness of his accusation. Slow, burning tears began to trickle from her eyes, and that only made her as furious with herself as she was with him. "Are you blaming me for this fiasco?"

His pride was stung by her sarcastic reference to their lovemaking, and a low growl erupted from his throat. "The fault is mine."

"Oh, that makes me feel heaps better!"

She managed to settle the straps on her shoulders, but her fingers were shaking too badly for her to get a grip on the zipper behind her. With a sob of mingled frustration and rage, she muttered, "You may not want to touch me, but you're going to have to force yourself, Donovan. You got me out of this dress in the first place, so you can damn well help me into it again!"

He did so with grim-lipped efficiency, all the while castigating himself for the mess he'd made of things. He had done the one thing he had promised himself never to do, and now Shannon was paying the price for his stupid loss of self-control. It was no wonder she was infuriated by his callous behavior. He was having just as much difficulty accepting what he had done to her.

He could live with her anger, he decided, but not with the anguished pain he had heard in her voice. He deserved to be consigned straight to Hades, but he knew Shannon was more likely asking herself what she had done to deserve such despicable treatment. Her head was bowed, but the rigidity of her spine testified to the control she was exerting over herself. Although he admired the inherent pride visible in her attempt at composure, he wished she would yell and scream and call him an insensitive bastard to his face. At least then he might be able to utter the words of remorse and guilt that were tearing at his throat.

But she didn't say another word, and eventually he couldn't bear the silence any longer. "You deserve an apology," he admitted abruptly.

Shannon wiped at her cheeks with the back of her hands and shook her head. Her low tones heavy with strain, she whispered, "Can we just leave now, please?"

Hesitantly he reached out and placed his fingers against the soft flesh of her upper arm. "Not until you've given me a chance to explain."

Her skin seemed to burn where he touched her. She shrugged her shoulder, and was relieved when his hand fell away. "What is there to explain?" She waved her hand in a gesture that encompassed the midnight sky and the deserted stretch of beach. "All of this is like something out of a dream, and I got a little carried away by the romantic atmosphere.''

"So did I.''

The laugh she attempted held the same flat inflection as her voice, and it was just as brittle. ''Don't try to save my dignity at this late date, please. I don't need your pity.''

"Pity?'' he raged, his eyes registering shock. ''The only person I'm feeling sorry for right now is myself. I'm the one who tried to seduce you and caused this mess.''

She closed her eyes, shutting out the sight of his thunderous frown. She was mentally and physically exhausted, and she was certainly in no condition to endure the postmortem he seemed to expect. ''Go ahead and play the martyr, but don't expect me to go along with you. I'm a grown woman, not a child, and as such I am just as responsible for my actions as you are for yours. You did not seduce me, Donovan. I was quite embarrassingly eager, and you reacted as any normal man would under the circumstances.''

He was aggravated beyond bearing by her cool attempt to categorize logically what had just happened between them. ''You make what happened between us sound like a lecture on basic biology.''

Shannon lifted her head, and her eyes were steady as she looked at him. ''Wasn't it?''

"Like hell,'' he snapped derisively. ''If I had only been driven by animal instinct, I'd be inside you right now!''

Hot color stained her cheeks, and she stared at a point beyond his shoulder. ''I don't want to discuss this any longer.''

"We have to.'' He reached for her hands, which were clasped tightly together in her lap, and covered them with one of his own. ''I don't want tonight to stand out in your mind as a shameful memory when you leave. I...I value your friendship too much to just chuck it away needlessly, Shannon.''

Her eyes widened in consternation, and a flicker of her earlier anger reappeared. "You can try lying to yourself, but what just happened had nothing to do with friendship. Not on my part, anyway. I wanted you, and I did my damnedest to make you want me. Obviously I failed miserably to meet your exalted standards for lovemaking, but for me my actions were an honest expression of my emotions. If that wasn't enough for you, then—"

"You think you disappointed me?" he burst out incredulously. "Where in heaven's name did you get such a crazy—"

"It wouldn't be the first time that's happened to me," she said, interrupting. "I was engaged once. Believe me, I ended up being a big disappointment to my fiancé. Of course, when Frank jilted me and married his perfect woman, he wasn't high on my list, either."

Shannon couldn't bear to tell him the entire truth, since baring her soul to that extent would shatter what little control she had left. Withdrawing mentally from the entire conversation, she shrugged her shoulders in attempted nonchalance. "It was a long time ago, and has nothing to do with us."

His eyes flashed fire. "The hell it doesn't, if you think I pulled back because I wasn't turned on enough by you to finish what I started!"

"What else am I supposed to think?"

Her expression had turned sullen, but her voice betrayed the pain he had inadvertently caused her. Tightening his grip over her hands, he jerked her forward until she was balancing her weight over a portion of his anatomy that was still hard and aching for what it had been denied. "Does this feel like the body of a man who doesn't want you?" he demanded. "Does it, Shannon?"

She jerked her hand back as though it had caught fire, and he smiled grimly. So much for her woman-of-the-world act, he thought, grasping her chin with forceful fingers before she could scramble away from him. "The first time I laid eyes on you I wanted you, woman! That's the Lord's own truth, and that need has grown in me until you're all I can think about anymore. How I've been able to keep my hands off you for this long is a mystery to me."

"Then why—?" She made a silencing gesture with her hand and quickly averted her eyes. "Never mind."

He chose to answer her unfinished question. "Because for a woman like you, sharing a man's bed would mean an emotional involvement."

"Don't most women—or men, for that matter—need to at least like their sexual partners?" she countered heatedly. "Or are you going to tell me that hopping into bed with total strangers is the norm?"

His eyes eloquent with frustration, he exhaled heavily. "It wasn't an unusual scenario in some of the bars I visited in my youth, but today that kind of behavior can get you killed. Anyway," he interjected with an irritated wave of his hand, "you're missing the point. Maybe we can get back on track if I became a touch more personal."

Shannon didn't like the sound of that. She had already let him dig deeper into her psyche than was wise, and pretending to a sophistication she didn't possess was becoming more difficult by the minute. Yet any retreat at this point was unthinkable, and she bravely kept her eyes trained on his unrevealing features. With a curt nod, she muttered, "By all means, let's get personal."

Donovan smiled at her sarcasm, but there wasn't much amusement in the eyes that searched hers so intently. "How many lovers have you had since your engagement was broken?"

She gasped. "That's none of your business!"

His gaze unrelenting, he lifted his other hand to her face. Gently he traced her cheekbones with his thumbs, while his fingers circled her slender neck. "How many, Shannon?"

Although the demand was whispered, it was harsh enough to make her jump. "None, but that doesn't mean..."

"And how many men have tried to get you into bed?" he asked, a note of triumph in his voice. "One...two...?"

She remained stubbornly silent, and he answered for her. "My guess is that quite a few guys have come on to you."

She pushed his hands aside and sat back on her heels. As if placing a little distance between them released her vocal cords, she asked, "And if they have?"

"You have all the normal urges," he remarked dryly. "Why didn't you have sex with any of them?"

Her remaining patience collapsed with the suddenness of a pricked balloon, and she shouted, "Because I didn't care for any of them!"

"That's the point I was trying to make," he said. "You couldn't handle a brief, no-strings affair, Shannon. When it ended, you'd be one of the walking wounded, and I don't want to see you hurt like that."

She jerked her head away from his touch and glared at him with rising indignation. "Surely whether or not I engage in an affair is for me to decide!"

His searching eyes narrowed on her rebellious features. "You'll be leaving the shelter a week from tomorrow, and I'm not going to ask you to stay beyond that time. Under those circumstances, do you still want us to become lovers?"

"You make it sound so cold-blooded," she murmured in dismay.

"I'm only telling it like it is, honey. Marriage doesn't figure into my plans, and it never will."

"So that's it!" she gasped incredulously. "You see me as a threat to your bachelor life-style!"

Jumping to her feet, she backed as far away from him as the rocks would allow. When he followed her, she wanted to strike at him with her clenched fists, but she decided on a scathing tongue as her best means of defense. With a defi-

ant toss of her head, she snapped, "Well, you needn'
worry. I'm not out for a marriage proposal, from you or any
other man. It may astonish you to learn this, but not al
women see a wedding ring in their futures."

He shook his head, his features set in lines of stubborn
ness. "You're deliberately misinterpreting this conversa
tion, Shannon."

"It seems to me you were trying to be insulting, or did i
just turn out that way?"

He raked an unsteady hand through his hair, his eyes
broodingly intent on her face. "I'm trying to be honest with
you, and you stand there and accuse me of insulting you. By
God, a guy can't win for losing with a woman!"

Shannon saw the confusion in his eyes, accompanied by
a flicker of pain that suddenly diffused her anger. She remembered seeing that same look on his face when he had
talked of his parents and their reason for conceiving him.
The first woman in his life had practically sold him to his
grandfather, and those who had followed her had probably
been just as concerned with material gain.

It wasn't difficult to understand why this man should feel
the need to place such strong defensive barriers around
himself, and she should have taken that into consideration
before jumping to conclusions. The trouble was, she was
just as guilty of hiding behind defensive barriers as he was.

For years her broken engagement and her loss of confidence in herself as a woman had colored her attitude toward men, and tonight she had let the same insecurities
affect her judgment. It had hurt her to realize that Donovan felt the need to protect himself from her, so she had
lashed out at him in a blind attempt to salvage her pride.

She slumped against the cold, hard rock behind her and
crossed her arms over her chest. The wind had picked up
sometime in the past few minutes, and she was suddenly
aware of the chill in the sea-moistened air. "I do appreciate

your honesty, Donovan, and I apologize for losing my temper."

Her chattering teeth did nothing to disguise the despondent note in her voice. With a muttered curse, he grabbed the car cover and shook it free of sand. Folding the bulky edges into a more manageable shape, he placed it around her shoulders. "Come on," he urged impatiently. "Let's get out of here before you freeze to death. I've got more than enough on my conscience as it is, and I don't need to add negligent homicide to the list."

Five

Shannon was seated at the long pine table in the kitchen, her head bent as she stared blankly at the menu plan in front of her. For once she was alone, and she was grateful for the unexpected moment of solitude. It gave her a chance to collect her thoughts and try to figure out how she was going to survive with her sanity intact until she left here at the end of the week.

Donovan was avoiding her. Sunday had passed without a single visit from him, and she had unsuccessfully tried to convince herself that he was just busy. When Monday followed the same pattern and she had only caught brief glimpses of him from a distance, she had been forced to face the truth. He had made up his mind regarding their relationship, and nothing was going to change it. He was going to save her from herself, and to hell with what she wanted.

She wanted Donovan, and thoughts of him were driving her crazy! No matter how hard she tried, she couldn't get the stupid, quixotic fool out of her mind. How could she, when her current surroundings were such an inescapable part of the man? Lancaster House *was* Donovan. It was his heart and soul. This place was more than an inanimate structure, she thought, and the realization filled her with pride in his achievements.

He had successfully trained his staff to blend efficiency with a caring, noninstitutionalized approach to the difficulties they faced with the kids they housed beneath their roof. As a result, the shelter was able to provide a warm, stable atmosphere for its inhabitants, which was essential for the mental and emotional well-being of the youngsters who were cared for here on a permanent basis.

This place was their home, and they treated it as such. There were necessary rules to follow and chores to be done, but that was true in any home environment. The only other thing Donovan asked of them was that they continue their education, which they seemed to do willingly enough. Of course, their affection for him went a long way toward oiling the wheels of progress, and it hadn't taken her long to realize that even the toughest and most streetwise of the kids had an unshakable respect for the shelter's founder.

She remembered her first evening at Lancaster House, which had been spent listening to stories about Donovan. One of the boys had talked about the night a transient had pulled a knife and brandished it about in an attempt to impress his audience. Unaware of the older man's Special Forces training in hand-to-hand combat, the youth had been disarmed and lying flat on his back before anyone even saw Donovan move.

When she asked what happened to the assailant, the youngster telling the story stared at her while the others laughed uproariously. His name was T.J. Although his dark eyes had held a wealth of worldly knowledge that she found abhorrent in one so young, and his voice verged on being surly, the admiration on his face was unmistakable when he replied, "Donovan kicked my butt and gave me another chance. Whattaya think, lady?"

"He didn't make you leave?" she questioned softly.

Another boy nudged T.J. in the side, earning a dirty look in the process. "Naw," he answered for T.J. "The lion made him clean toilets for a month."

A second round of raucous laughter ensued, and this time Shannon joined in. As soon as she could catch her breath, she asked, "What was that you called him, Paco?"

"The lion," he replied with another snicker.

Although she thought she knew the answer, she asked, "Why?"

Rolling his eyes toward the heavens, he said, "You'll find out if you stay around here for long."

And she had! The nickname had little to do with his thick, overly long mane of sandy hair and his golden cat's eyes, and everything to do with his impatient disposition. Donovan Lancaster was an extremely vocal man when irritated, and quite often he prowled the building, roaring at the top of his lungs, when his temper was aroused.

And sometimes when it wasn't, she amended as she stifled a smile. The kids and his staff did little more than wince, sometimes grin, and calmly go on about their business when the lion exercised his lungs. Shannon had quickly learned to do the same. God, how she missed the sound of his surly growl!

The brisk tapping of heels against the hardwood floor of the hall caught her attention, and she glanced up to see Tricia Everett framed in the doorway. Her smile was friendly, and the teal blue two-piece linen suit she wore gave added depth to her sparkling eyes and made Shannon feel scruffier than usual. "Hi," she said as she stepped forward. "I see you're still alive."

"And kicking," Shannon retorted with a laugh. Rising to her feet, she gestured toward the large electric coffee urn on the counter behind her and lifted an inquiring brow.

"I'd love a cup," Tricia confessed on a moan. "I've been run off my feet most of the morning, and the pot in my office decided to gurgle a dying lament yesterday."

Plopping herself down at the table with little regard for her delicate hosiery, Tricia mused, "Or was it the day before?"

Shannon's lips quirked wryly. "Does it matter?"

"Not so you'd notice." Accepting a full earthenware mug from her newest friend, Tricia inhaled the steamy aroma and asked, "Is Donovan around? I wanted to speak to him about one of the kids he sent to my group session last Wednesday night."

Shannon had heard about the counseling sessions Tricia held one evening a week for individuals from both this shelter and her sister-in-law Maria's nonprofit organization. With the time she donated to Donovan's kids and to FACES, Shannon wondered how she also managed to maintain a private practice.

Already having been given a good example of how perceptive Tricia could be where her fellow man—or in her case, woman—was concerned, Shannon kept her eyes on the coffee mug in her hand as she returned to her seat. Although she tried to respond to Tricia's question casually, the brittle, stilted sound of her voice gave her away. "I haven't seen him, but I'm sure he's around here somewhere. Would you like me to send someone to find him?"

Tricia tapped a lacquered fingernail on the oilcloth-covered table and waited for Shannon to look at her. When she did so, with visible reluctance, a finely penciled brow rose in a questioning arc. "Is something bothering you, Shannon?"

There was such a wealth of commiseration in those wide blue eyes, Shannon found herself blurting out the truth before she was aware of having done so. "Not unless you count a certain stupid, self-righteous, egocentric, foul-tempered individual I prefer not to mention by name."

Tricia shook her head and leaned her elbow on the table with a long-suffering sigh. Cradling her head on her hand, she muttered glumly, "I was afraid of this. I just knew if I left it up to Donovan he'd blow it."

Shannon's mouth flew open, and she gazed across the distance separating them suspiciously. "Left what up to him?"

"Romance—what else?" she retorted in disgust. "The man's a blind menace when it comes to women."

Putting her coffee down, Shannon pushed aside her notebook and plopped her own elbows on the shiny-clean surface of the table. Resting her chin on fisted hands, she nodded in agreement. "You've got that one right," she grumbled. "He is a living, breathing contradiction walking around on two legs."

Tricia grinned. "How so?"

"First he starts making passionate love to me," Shannon stated tersely, "and then he informs me that we aren't going to have an affair. I, of course, have no say in the matter. Now he's avoiding me, an evasive maneuver which makes me want to wring his neck. I would, too, but there's no sense in both of us suffering from a guilty conscience."

With a grimace, Tricia admitted, "That sounds like Donovan."

Shannon continued her indignant tirade with barely a pause for breath. "You don't know the half of it," she countered in disgust. "Even if I wanted to have an affair with him—not saying I do, mind you, but even if I did—it would be impossible to accomplish long-distance. And since he has so cavalierly decided to save me from my weak-minded little self, that's just what he's counting on."

This time it was Tricia's mouth that opened wide on a gasp, which was quickly followed by a gleeful squeal. "I knew I was right! When I saw the way he was eyeing you at the christening party last Saturday, I had a feeling you were the one who could break through that wall of reserve he hides behind.''

Considering what she had just admitted to Tricia, Shannon didn't see what the other woman had to be so ecstatic about. Donovan had made it clear that he wanted nothing more to do with her. He wanted her gone, vanished, out of his life for good. There was probably another woman he hadn't told her about, she decided despondently, some sophisticated, gorgeous female who knew how to conduct an affair properly. Someone he preferred over her.

She said as much to Tricia, only to have her respond with a negative shake of her head. ''Donovan doesn't play around with people's emotions, Shannon. He's been hurt like that too often himself.''

''He told me a little about his background,'' she admitted. ''His grandfather sounded like a cold, manipulative old buzzard.''

Tricia's eyes widened in shock. ''I'm surprised he talked about him at all. He doesn't usually discuss his family or his past with anyone. Did he mention his parents?''

Shannon nodded, and Tricia gave a snort of derision. ''If you want my opinion, those two were the ones who perfected emotional cruelty to a fine art. There are many forms of child abuse other than the physical, and emotional neglect certainly qualifies. What really makes me angry is knowing that they're still feeding off Donovan like leeches.''

Although the words nearly stuck in her throat, Shannon attempted to pacify the other woman. ''In their own way, maybe they do care about him.''

Tricia's mouth curled in disgust, and her eyes flashed. ''They never gave a damn about their son, Shannon. Not when he was a child, and certainly not now. Lancaster senior even tried to get the will overturned, but the courts upheld Donovan's claim. From what I've observed since, his mother and father only come around when they want an advance on the allowance the old man provided for them.''

Shannon's features reflected her distress. "Poor, lonely man," she whispered. "He hasn't had much love in his life, has he, Tricia? No wonder he finds it impossible to trust in his emotions—or anyone else's, for that matter."

"I'm glad you realize that," Tricia said, her eyes shadowed with worry. She leaned closer to Shannon. "Donovan would never deliberately hurt you, but he may not be able to help it."

"I know," Shannon responded, her soft voice filled with sadness. "He doesn't trust himself not to hurt me, and I don't think he can trust me not to hurt him, either, Tricia."

Tricia agreed with a silent inclination of her head. "As you said, Donovan's not used to trusting other people. His only real commitment is to this shelter and the welfare of his kids, but he deserves so much more from life, Shannon. Inside, he's one of the loneliest people I've ever known, and yet he always holds back from any real intimacy. Even old friends like me find it difficult to get past his barriers."

Shannon was quick to reassure her. "It's obvious he cares a great deal for you. He told me that you and your family have given him the only real affection he's ever known."

"But it isn't enough," Tricia said hollowly. "I've prayed that someday he'd meet a woman like you, but now that he has, I'm concerned with the future. He might not be willing to risk a serious involvement, Shannon."

"He admitted as much to me himself," Shannon responded quickly. "He made certain I understood that marriage didn't figure in his plans. At the time, the admission infuriated me. Now that I've had time to think, I realize he was right about me. I already...care a great deal for him, and if we became lovers... Well, let's just say that an affair between us would put the kind of emotional pressure on him that he isn't prepared to deal with."

"That's because he's never been seriously involved with a woman before, and like any sensible, intelligent human being, he's afraid of the unknown." Tricia's brows furrowed. Her expression was thoughtful as she added, "But if he bothered to warn you off, and he really is avoiding you, maybe his feelings already go deeper than he's prepared to admit."

Shannon would have liked to think so, but it wasn't a supposition to which she could respond unemotionally. So all she said was, "Being an honorable man, he wasn't about to take his pleasure at my expense. Although I don't take well to rejection or appreciate having decisions that affect my life made for me, I have to respect his good intentions."

"Good intentions be damned, that guy needs a clout on the noggin," Tricia retorted indignantly. "It's no wonder there have only been good-time bimbos and social-climbing groupies in his past. He doesn't know how to relate to a decent woman, and it's about time someone taught him."

Shannon wrapped suddenly cold hands around her coffee mug, and studied the remaining contents with a dull, lackluster gaze. In a voice that held more longing than she was aware of, she murmured, "I'm drawn to Donovan like to no other man I've ever known, but he's such a complex individual, he frightens me, Tricia. I'm not certain I could give him what he needs, even if he was prepared to let me try."

Shannon heard the other woman's breath catch, and glanced up to find Tricia studying her features intently. "I'm afraid you're going to prove heavy on my conscience, my friend."

Shannon's mouth was firm with annoyance. "Oh, not another one! What am I, some kind of guiltmonger?"

Tricia giggled. "You're a very nice woman, and I should be shot for throwing you in at the deep end without first finding out if you could swim."

Tricia wasn't alluding to water sports, and Shannon's laughter had a hollow ring. "You could have tied stones to my feet, and I would have jumped in anyway."

"Is that supposed to make me feel better?"

"You needn't worry," Shannon said, her voice rife with irony. "I may not have had much practical experience, but I'll manage to keep my head above water unless Donovan pushes me under."

"Don't give up without a struggle," Tricia urged her as she rose to her feet. "Whether he knows it or not, Donovan needs you to care for him, Shannon."

For a long time after Tricia left, Shannon sat staring into space, a certain tawny-haired, golden-eyed man the only thing on her mind.

The following day marked the middle of the work week, and by late afternoon Shannon had mentally dubbed her surroundings Hell's Kitchen. The Bay Area was sweltering from record high temperatures for late September, and the air-conditioning had sputtered and died somewhere around midmorning.

She was hot and tired and thoroughly frustrated, but she would have let herself melt into a puddle on the tile floor before complaining to Donovan. She might have sent one of the other kids to do the complaining, but they had taken one of the vans to their counseling session with Tricia. Sam and Trina had taken the other, and when Donovan discovered where they had gone, he was going to hit the roof.

Oh, well, she decided fatalistically, she'd get around to telling him eventually. Right now, she was all by herself, with only a bunch of chicken carcasses for company, which was probably for the best. Between the heat, worrying about life in general and Trina and Sam in particular, and too many nights spent tossing and turning in her narrow bed, she wasn't in the best condition for serious conversation.

In fact, when it came to growling, she could probably give the lion a run for his money. She grinned at the thought, then grimaced when a drop of sweat trickled down her throat and disappeared between her breasts. She had dressed this morning in a loose pair of jogging shorts and an equally roomy cotton shirt, and both were sticking to her like glue.

With equally sticky hands, she brushed flour from the enveloping bib apron she wore and absentmindedly noted that the cover-up hadn't done much to protect her yellow shorts and sleeveless top from being liberally dusted. Tiredly she wiped a hand across her sweat-moistened forehead and glared toward the two industrial-size stoves located along the far wall.

They seemed to glare right back at her, which wasn't surprising, considering her current frame of mind. During the daylight hours and long into the evening, the surfaces of those mammoth metal monsters were covered by gigantic cast-iron pots that disgorged fragrant wisps of steam into the already humid atmosphere. She could sure use the air-conditioning, she thought longingly.

Sprinkling water on a glob of dough spread out on the big cutting board in front of her, she attacked the sticky mass with renewed enthusiasm. Tearing a piece off, she began shaping it into a ball with more force than finesse. Others followed, and while her hands worked her mind once again wandered in an irritatingly familiar direction.

Donovan. Tricia was right—the man was a menace when it came to women. What he knew about the fairer sex could be written on the head of a pin, and a rusty one at that. He had aroused her desire and then nipped it in the bud with ruthless determination. How dare he make such a decision for both of them, and then hide from her like a sniveling coward? What did he think she was going to do? she wondered peevishly. Jump his bones when he wasn't looking?

And if she was given the opportunity, wouldn't she do that very thing? Hadn't the past three nights of mental and physical turmoil proved how much she wanted him, regardless of the limits he chose to impose on their relationship? Donovan had found a place in her heart with appalling ease, so the damage to that internal organ had already been done. Whether she slept with him or not would make little difference, and forgetting him would be impossible.

Until she had met that lion-maned, grim-featured male, she hadn't known the true meaning of the phrase *sexual attraction*. Now she understood why it had been so easy for her to avoid intimate relationships with other men, she thought. It had nothing to do with frigidity—of which she'd been accused on a couple of occasions—and everything to do with lack of chemistry. There was certainly nothing lacking when it came to Donovan.

He made her all hot and bothered just by looking at her, inducing a bone-melting reaction of which she would never have believed herself capable. But along with his physical appeal, there was his emotional appeal to contend with. He had an inner strength she admired, and a lonely vulnerability she shared. His drive and his dedication to duty matched her own. He was not selfish, and he was not prone to insensitivity to others. Except possibly to her, she amended with a scowl.

In fact, he was everything she had ever hoped to find in a man, in those faraway days when she had still been able to dream of happy-ever-afters. But those days were long gone, she thought sadly. She and Donovan had been altered by time and circumstances into the people they now were, and both of them were wary of placing their trust in others. She didn't see how it would ever be possible for them to bridge the tremendous gap their individual pain had placed between them, but at least she was willing to try.

Donovan wasn't, and realizing that he was trying to protect her by keeping his distance didn't lessen her longing to be with him. It also didn't do much to alleviate her frustration, or diminish the irritation his pigheadedness was causing her to feel toward him. She blew a limp strand of hair off her forehead in exasperation, wishing a certain man was as easy to push back into line.

As she grabbed hold of the cutting board, with its moun-
tainous pile of dough balls, she realized it was heavier than
she anticipated. She managed to lug it to the other side of
the kitchen, but she thought her arms would fall off in the
process. With a grateful moan, she released her burden on
top of the scratched Formica countertop, that formed a di-
vider between the two stoves. Two large cast-iron pots were
simmering on one, and a third on the other.

She had decided to make an expanded version of chicken
and dumplings for dinner, with plenty of fresh vegetables to
round out the meal. Sniffing the air, she began dropping
dough balls by hand into the mixture. She only hoped dinner tasted as good as it smelled. She was proud of the hearty,
nutritious meals she provided for the shelter, which could
stand the test of being left warming on the stove for hours.

Not that her absent employer would be around tonight to
test her culinary efforts, she deduced sourly. Shifting her
attention to the second pot on the stove, she began to add
the dumplings absentmindedly. Her imagination superim-
posed Donovan's face on each white glob, and just the
thought of boiling him in chicken broth was therapeutic.
With a lighter heart, she slid the cutting board along the
countertop until it was in line with the stove on her left, and
placed the last of the dumplings in the third bubbling pot.

"Damn, it's like a blast furnace in here!" a deep voice
growled from behind her.

With a startled yelp, Shannon jumped, nearly knocking
the empty cutting board to the floor as she whirled to face
the fiercely frowning man who was taking up most of the
doorway. He was dressed in a pair of faded jeans and a
short-sleeved blue shirt that was unbuttoned to the middle
of his chest, and her mouth went dry at the sight of him.
Those tight pants seemed to cling to his muscular thighs with
loving intimacy, leaving her in no doubt that beneath the
heavy denim was a body to die for.

Shannon quickly lifted her gaze to a safer location. Unfortunately for her erratic pulse rate, her eyes didn't get any farther than the broad, well developed chest she remembered so well. His darkly tanned flesh was already beginning to glisten in the steamy kitchen atmosphere, and she swallowed with difficulty. The silky mat of brownish-gold body hair, much darker than that on his head, that began just below his collarbone, trailed down to the last button on his gaping shirt.

Her imagination followed it even further, past the silver snap on his jeans, to where it formed a concealing nest at the juncture of his thighs. The vivid mental picture nearly caused her to strangle on her next breath, and she silently ordered her mind to behave itself. Taking the coward's way out, she lowered her gaze to her dough-encrusted hands. Nervously wiping them on a damp rag, she muttered, "I've gotten used to the heat."

"Dammit, there was no need to suffer in silence, Shannon. Why didn't you ask for some fans to be installed in here?" Donovan eyed her speculatively and added, "For that matter, why haven't you reported the faulty air-conditioning unit?"

Shannon's spine stiffened at the sarcastic inflection in his voice, and her chin rose in silent defiance. "You haven't been around to ask or report to, Donovan."

No, he hadn't, he reminded himself guiltily, as he noted the tired, dispirited droop to her lovely mouth, and the mauve shadows visible beneath her eyes. Even the freckles dusting her nose seemed more prominent than usual. Although her cheeks were rosy from the heat, he wasn't fooled by that hectic rush of color. Shannon was exhausted, and his neglect of her tore at the facade of indifference he had tried to maintain between them for the last few days. If he hadn't been avoiding her like a snare-shy rabbit, he thought with self-directed anger, he would have seen for himself that she was doing too much.

For God's sake, what had he been thinking of? He should have taken better care of her. She was conscientious to a fault, and not only where her kitchen duties were concerned. On numerous occasions he had seen how unreservedly she gave time and attention to anyone who needed her, without counting the cost to herself. If he wasn't careful, this damn place was going to wear her out even more quickly than he had anticipated.

His gaze encompassed the otherwise empty room, and his frown shifted into an expression of consternation. Where was everybody? he wondered. The predinner hour was usually the kitchen's busiest time of day, which was why he had chosen to approach Shannon now. He shifted uneasily, and raked his hair off his forehead with an unsteady hand. So much for meeting on neutral ground, he thought sardonically, with plenty of people around to cramp any amorous impulses.

Trina was especially protective of Shannon, and he knew she wouldn't have left her to manage alone. Shannon was rapidly becoming the girl's role model, which was hardly surprising, under the circumstances. Trina's mother had died when she was barely old enough to remember her, and all she had ever known from her father was drunkenness and abusive behavior.

Not that Trina was alone in her growing affection for Shannon, he reminded himself with a surge of pride. Half the kids in this place would roll over and play dead if a certain redhead asked them to. How could anyone resist her appeal? he asked himself. She radiated a warmth and a generosity of spirit that could pierce the hide of the devil himself, let alone a bunch of youths who were lonely and hurt and aching for someone to care. Just as he was, he realized with a sense of shocked awareness. Just as he had always been.

The heavy silence that had fallen between them was making Shannon feel like jumping right out of her skin. With forced bravado she asked, "Was there something you wanted, Donovan?"

Donovan wanted *her,* and he had spent the past few days in a frustrating hell of his own making. Even working himself half to death hadn't prevented him constantly craving the sight and sound and touch of her. Which was why he had finally surrendered to his weakness, only to find a wilted facsimile of the woman he had planted in this damn hothouse!

With a muttered exclamation, he swept his arm in an expansive gesture that encompassed the entire kitchen, and ignored her question to ask a couple of his own. "You're supposed to have help in here. Where is Trina, and wasn't Sam on the roster for kitchen duty this week?"

Mention of the teens brought a gentle smile to Shannon's lips, but her eyes were suddenly filled with consternation as she acknowledged his angry mood. Clearing her throat uneasily, she admitted, "I should have talked to you about Trina."

His eyes narrowed as he studied her apprehensive features. "What's wrong?"

"Nothing! I mean—" Her voice gave out on a squeak, and she once again cleared her throat and stiffened her spine. Glancing at him with wavering resolution, she inhaled a fortifying breath. "I gave her this afternoon off."

"Now why would you do that?" His gaze swept her tense figure, and there was a marked note of derision in his voice. "Especially since you're the one who looks to be in need of a break."

"Oh, I—I'm fine. And Trina had a-an appointment she needed to keep."

Immediately alerted by her stammering evasiveness, his brows lifted in a querying arc. "What appointment was that, Shannon?"

"Well, it wasn't e-exactly an appointment."

He wasn't the most patient of men under the best of circumstances, and this beating around the bush wasn't improving his temper any. "Then suppose you tell me—exactly—where Trina is right now?"

Drawing in a quick breath, Shannon closed her eyes and blurted out the truth. Then she calmly waited for the sound of the lion's furious roar to shake the walls and rattle the windows.

Six

Donovan didn't disappoint her. "She went to see a what?" he yelled.

Shannon's eyes popped open, and she watched him approach with a stiff-legged stride that didn't bode well for her hopes of a calm, rational discussion of Trina's problem. When he paused directly in front of her, she backed into the hard edge of the countertop and whispered, "A film about the Lamaze method of natural childbirth."

Donovan looked thunderstruck. "She's pregnant?" he questioned hoarsely. "How far along?"

"Nearly f-four months."

An unmistakable flicker of emotion showed in the depths of his eyes. "Why in the hell didn't she tell me?"

Shannon felt a sudden urge to cry at the pain and bewilderment in his voice. In an attempt to console him, she said, "Trina hid her condition from everyone, not just you."

"The fact remains, she didn't trust me enough to confide in me."

"Of course she trusts you," she countered swiftly.

"Then why didn't she come to me?"

"She didn't exactly broadcast the news to me, either, Donovan." Her lips curved wryly. "I'm a nurse, and when she exhibited certain signs, I had my suspicions. Then she fainted a few days ago, and she admitted the truth when I questioned her. I think she was relieved to have another woman to discuss her condition with. She hadn't had her pregnancy confirmed by a doctor yet, and she was frightened and worried about the baby's well-being."

Donovan was concerned, too. "We'll have to set up an appointment at Fairmont right away, Shannon. I want her to have the best prenatal care possible."

"I agree. In fact, I—"

He gave a wave of his hand, his expression distracted enough for her to realize he wasn't conscious of having interrupted her. "Trina's not as healthy as I'd like her to be," he admitted worriedly. "She was in a pretty sorry state when she showed up here a year ago, raging with fever and as weak as a kitten. But even as sick as she was, she was still stubborn enough to give me grief over seeing a doctor. I had to practically hog-tie her to get her into the county clinic. She doesn't trust our public health care system. I know she preferred taking her chances on the streets, rather than in the orphanage the welfare sent her to after she proved disruptive in foster care."

Shannon paused to smile at him with approval. "Trina told me how good you were to her, and how you cleared it with the authorities so she could stay here on a permanent basis and stop hiding."

"I just went with her to court when she filed for emancipation, to testify that she had a job and a roof over her head. It was no big deal."

"I think it was a very big deal," she countered softly.

Embarrassed by the admiration he heard in her voice, he muttered, "Trina's a good kid who's had some tough breaks. She works for her room and board and the small salary I give her. I don't provide a free ride for anyone, so quit looking at me like that, Shannon."

Her mouth formed a gentle curve. "You sound almost defensive, Donovan. Why is that, I wonder? Could it be that the big, tough man really does have the heart of a pussycat, as Tricia once suggested?"

"I just don't want you getting the wrong idea," he said stiffly. "The few kids who are asked to stay here longer than a couple of nights at a time have earned my respect, otherwise I wouldn't lift a finger to help them. Believe me, my motives are mainly self-serving."

He gave a negligent shrug of his shoulders and averted his gaze to the window over the sink. "This place requires a lot of care and supervision, as you've had time to realize. I need all the help I can get, and working here keeps the kids off the streets and out of trouble. One hand washes the other, so to speak. So don't start imagining me as some kind of benevolent jerk with a halo over my head."

Shannon knew very well that Donovan was spouting a lot of nonsense. His staff was large and quite competent, and the jobs he provided for kids like Trina were superfluous. But all she said was "I wouldn't dare! Such admiration might give you a complex."

He gritted his teeth in exasperation. "Let's get back on track here. I guess the first order of business is finding a doctor for Trina, and she'd better not give me any arguments this time."

"You don't have to worry," she admitted, somewhat shamefacedly. "I drove her to the clinic yesterday, which was how we found out about the film being shown this afternoon. It explains Lamaze preparation and follows an actual birth. If she's interested, at the end of the film she can sign up for a class that's due to start in three months. The doctor said they fill up fast, and advised her to register early."

"God!" Donovan raked his fingers through his gold-streaked hair, his expression distracted. "This is a hell of a mess. Trina is barely sixteen, hardly more than a baby herself."

"That's why she hid her condition, Donovan. Even though the courts emancipated her, giving her adult status by law, you know how paranoid Trina is about the welfare authorities. She was afraid they would pressure her to give up her baby. I told her you wouldn't let anyone hassle her."

"You—?" He sucked air into his lungs, and released it in a startled whoosh. "You told her *what?*" he roared.

Shannon didn't even flinch. She kept her eyes steady and unwavering on his. He was such a phony, she thought, her entire being flooded with tenderness toward this gentle, caring man, whose bark was so much worse than his bite. His good, kind heart might be hidden inside his manly chest, but no one who knew him at all ever had cause to doubt its existence. Amusement lightening her voice, she said, "You heard what I said."

"Since when do you speak for me?" he questioned with ominous softness.

More to hide an unrepentant grin than anything else, she turned her back to him and began noisily searching the bottom cupboards. Withdrawing three bulky stainless-steel lids, she covered each of the bubbling pots on the two stoves and glanced at him over her shoulder. It was difficult to manage a reproving stare, but she managed to do so without bursting out laughing at his sour expression.

Frustrated as all hell, Donovan glowered down at her. "Aren't you going to answer me?"

"I don't see any need."

Calmly she lowered the stove settings to simmer, and slanted him a distinctly impertinent glance as he paused beside her. "You know you're going to do everything you can to help Trina keep her child, Donovan."

Closing his eyes, he slumped against the edge of the counter. "Damn straight!"

At the soft sound of her laughter, his lashes lifted, and he grinned sheepishly. But almost immediately his mouth firmed, and his forehead creased into a thoughtful frown. "Trina's been trimming my hair, and anyone else's she can get her hands on. She's good at it."

"She certainly had a lot of it to work with in your case," she commented, eyeing his leonine mane with a grin.

But Donovan obviously wasn't in the mood for levity, because her teasing remark flew right over his hairy head. "I know some people who might be willing to foster her and take care of the baby while she completes her education," he mused. "After she has her high school diploma, she could attend cosmetology classes. Do you think she'd like that, Shannon?"

Yes, and he would be the one to dip into his pockets to further the girl's education, she thought, her eyes tender as she watched him begin to pace in front of her. Back and forth he went, her kindhearted lion man. His head was bent, and his hands were clasped together behind his back, and his loping strides took him from one end of—

Her kindhearted lion man! *Hers?* Shannon straightened with a jerk, her eyes wide as she gazed into space in disbelief. She would admit to desiring Donovan, and even to being drawn to him emotionally, but the possessiveness in that last thought horrified her. What was happening here? she asked herself with inner sternness. The man belonged to no one but himself, and always would. If she'd had any doubts about that, his avoidance of her since Saturday night had certainly driven the point home. Had her good sense flown right out the window and joined the honking geese flying south for the winter?

"Do you think she'd like to train to be a hairdresser, Shannon?"

She refocused on their conversation with a mental shake of her head. "I think she'd rather marry Sam," she muttered distractedly.

"Sam's the father?" he ground out furiously. "And to think I asked him to look out for her! Wait until I get my hands on that dumb, irresponsible, oversexed little—"

Sam had been in and out of the shelter from the age of fourteen, and Donovan had had definite plans for the boy's future. Although she understood his disappointment in his protégé, she hurriedly interrupted his tirade with one of her own. Lifting a belligerent chin in his direction, she said, "Sam is over eighteen and fully capable of making his own decisions. And since Trina has been emancipated, might I remind you that she doesn't need your approval to marry?"

"But that doesn't mean marriage is the most sensible course for them to follow." He shook his head in exasperation. "They're so damnably young, Shannon."

"Yes, but they're both trying to face their responsibilities in an adult manner," she told him gently. "You have to give them credit for that much, Donovan."

Instead of agreeing with her, he ran his hands through his hair and slumped against the edge of the counter. "You know as well as I do how little chance their relationship has of surviving this kind of pressure."

Shannon nodded, the sadness in her eyes mirroring his own. "All we can do is hope for the best and give them our love and support."

Donovan's expression hardened. "Sam wants to become an engineer. Did you know that, Shannon? He had his future all planned out. Two years of junior college, followed by university. He figured if he kept his grade point average high enough, he could earn several scholarships to finance his continued education. He didn't want to be stuck in a dead-end job he hated, or in prison for dealing drugs, like his father and brothers. With the responsibility of a wife and baby, what chance does he have now of realizing his dreams?

"And Trina should be enjoying high school with other girls her age, going to dances and parties instead of changing diapers and making formula. Dammit to hell, a baby is a huge responsibility, both financially and emotionally. They never had a chance to be children, and now they're going to have to raise one themselves. In the name of heaven, why weren't those young fools more careful?"

"Apportioning blame at this stage is senseless, Donovan."

Venting his frustration and disappointment on Shannon was just as senseless, but Donovan found himself doing so with great enthusiasm. He ridiculed her sensible attitude, and criticized her calmness in the face of disaster. He ranted and raved for a full minute, only to be halted by a slender finger being shaken under his nose. "You stop it this instant, Donovan Lancaster!"

Too surprised to do more than gape, he did as ordered, eyeing her warily. Nodding in satisfaction, she crossed her arms over her chest and nodded. "That's better," she murmured complacently. "If you're through pitching a fit, maybe we can concentrate on the best way to help Trina and Sam prepare for the difficulties they're going to have to face."

"In case it's escaped your notice, I have been trying to help them. For all the good it's done me," he tacked on sarcastically.

Although she understood his disappointment, Shannon was thoroughly out of patience with his belligerent attitude. Angling her chin defiantly, she placed her hands on her hips and returned his glare in full measure. "Sam and Trina didn't create this baby just to spite you, you know. The only thing they're guilty of is loving each other, however irresponsibly, and you should be proud of them for being willing to accept their responsibilities."

Donovan was dumbfounded by the tiny termagant who was standing up to him so vocally. He was not used to being told what he would and would not do, but oddly enough, he found her bossiness pleasing. Her flashing green eyes took his breath away, and he was barely managing to keep a grin off his face. She was really something when she got her dander up!

In an attempt to goad her further, he drawled, "Oh, I should, should I?"

"Yes, you should! Sam worships the ground you walk on, and he has enough to worry about now without having you growl at him like a castrated bear."

He winced visibly. "Ouch!"

A tiny smile spread across her mouth, and she peeked up at him through a thick fringe of lashes. "If the baby's a boy, they're going to name him Donovan."

He straightened awkwardly, his eyes alight with pleasure. "Where's Sam?" he asked gruffly.

With a return of her earlier evasiveness, she said, "Uh, he, um . . . borrowed the panel truck so he could take Trina to see the film."

He sighed and eyed her with resignation. "I'm not even going to ask who provided him with the keys."

She shot him a guilty look. "I'm sorry, Donovan. You were nice enough to suggest I use one of the shelter's vehicles if I needed transportation, but I had no right to loan it to Sam without your permission."

"If it makes you feel any better, I would have let him use it myself."

She expelled the air from her lungs in a relieved sigh that rapidly escalated into a yawn. Covering her mouth with her hand, she murmured a brief apology. "Was there anything else you wanted to speak to me about, Donovan? I'm through here until the dinner crowd starts trailing in, and a quick shower and a change of clothes sounds like my idea of heaven."

Angry with himself for having forgotten, even briefly, how tired she looked, he barely prevented himself from uttering the string of curses forming in his mind. "You're through here for the night."

Not at all pleased by his imperious manner, she decided an argument was in order. "Might I remind you of the rules you yourself set up for running the kitchen, Donovan? At least one person must be on duty to supervise when the stoves or ovens are in use, and tonight I'm that person. I don't know when Trina and Sam will be back, and my other kitchen aides are at Tricia's."

"I said, you're through here for the night!" Striding toward the doorway, he hollered, "Lopez!" at the top of his lungs.

At the name, Shannon stifled a groan of protest. Shannon had met the feisty, garrulous old man several times while enjoying her daily walks through the grounds. She had listened in fascination to his stories of Donovan when he was still in training pants, admittedly moved by the tales of a lonely little boy who had spent much of his time "helping" his friend work in the gardens.

And he had apparently been just as fascinated by her, she remembered with a distinct twinge of uneasiness. It hadn't taken her long to recognize his fierce love for and loyalty toward his employer. Nor had she been left in doubt as to his desire to find Donovan a wife. He could give Tricia a run for her money, she thought, wondering if there was something in the air out here that caused this propensity toward matchmaking.

Within seconds, the sound of sandaled feet shuffling against the hardwood flooring of the hallway could be heard, and a graying, stoop-shouldered man scurried into view. "You hollered, *niño?*"

Manuel Lopez was a good foot shorter than Donovan, and he was probably the only person alive brave enough to call him "boy" to his face. With the freedom their mutual affection gave them, the two men glared at each other. Finally Donovan shrugged in resignation and asked, "Can you take over in here for Shannon tonight?"

With a rheumy-eyed wink in her direction that made her flinch, the old man nodded. "You were the one who said I must take things more slowly. I did not need all those men to help me tend my plants, but you would not listen. Thanks to your fussing, I do not have enough to keep me busy. But you just remember, I do not take something for nothing, *niño. Nada!* A man has his pride, and—"

"You won't stay around and become a charity case." Donovan finished the familiar litany with an impatient scowl. "Now that you've taken the edge off your tongue, old man, can I count on you to maintain order in here?"

Lopez straightened as far as his arthritic bones allowed, and stomped past the younger man with an air of affronted dignity. But as he paused in front of Shannon, he grinned, displaying a gold-capped front tooth. "Like I told you, El Gato needs a woman to sweeten his temper." He let loose with a mirth-filled cackle, and his dark eyes danced wickedly. "You going to volunteer, *niña?*"

Shannon reacted to his question with a spirited toss of her head. "I don't have a suicidal bone in my body, Señor Lopez."

But two black-button eyes had noticed her softening features, and the laughter that burst from his lungs would have rivaled a hyena's in pitch. Hurriedly Shannon rushed past him, her cheeks on fire, to join Donovan in the hallway. As they moved toward the suite of rooms he had provided for her use, he glanced down at her and sighed in exasperation. "Manuel didn't mean to embarrass you, Shannon."

She gaped at him in dismay. "You heard?"

"Yes, although I probably would have guessed anyway," he admitted with a chuckle. "Even though he never married, Lopez is forever harping at me to give up my bachelor ways and settle down with a good woman. Actually, you should be flattered. He has very definite ideas about what qualities a good woman should possess."

"I'm sure he does," she managed to say in a strangled tone.

As they reached the door to her sitting room, he observed her heightened color with growing amusement. "You *are* embarrassed!"

"I am not!" Eyeing him with disfavor, she threw open the door and crossed the threshold in a rush. Much to her consternation, he followed her, and lowered himself into her overstuffed easy chair with the air of a man who planned on staying a while. "Don't you have work to do?" she questioned sarcastically.

Crossing his arms behind his head, he leaned back with a satisfied grunt. "Nope, and since you don't either, we might as well spend the evening together. We can eat dinner at my place." His eyes twinkled devilishly as he added, "My air-conditioner is in tip-top shape, and we could both use a little cooling off. Don't you agree?"

The invitation was surprising, given how adroitly he had been avoiding her these past few days. Although she was tempted to jump at the chance to spend the evening with him, she wasn't about to let him get away with taking her for granted. "I'm not hungry," she lied.

Studying her mutinous features with a smile, he murmured, "Go take your shower, honey. You might not be hungry, but personally, I'm starving. Whatever you had simmering in those pots smelled delicious."

Determined to be difficult, her lip pushed forward in a pout. "It's chicken and dumplings, and after smelling it all day, I think I'll pass."

"There's a Chinese take-out place nearby that delivers," he told her, his tone blatantly tempting. "Do you like Chinese food?"

Since that particular cuisine was one of her favorites, she decided she was cutting off her nose to spite her face. The unseasonable heat wave, coupled with brooding over Donovan, had savaged her appetite lately. But suddenly, probably due to the hopeful gleam in a pair of sensuous brown eyes, she was hungry enough to take a bite out of the nearest table leg. "How is their moo goo gai pan?" she asked meekly.

In lieu of an answer, he kissed the tips of his fingers and lifted his eyes skyward. Without saying another word, Shannon disappeared into her bedroom, and returned with a change of clothes cradled against her chest. She was breathless from rushing, but managed to reassure him as to her intent as she disappeared through the bathroom door. "I won't even wait for the water to get hot!"

With an appreciative grin, Donovan wandered over to the built-in shelving unit across the room and reached for the phone. Whistling under his breath as he dialed and waited for the restaurant to answer, he decided on Oriental gastronomic offerings that would send Shannon into ecstasies. Just the thought of Shannon in ecstasy caused his hand to shake, but he quickly convinced himself that this momentary weakness was caused by lack of sustenance.

Seven

What Donovan always referred to as his cottage turned out to be Shannon's dream of the perfect home. The early-evening weather was so balmy that they decided to walk the half mile from the shelter, and as they rounded the wooded copse, the large house appeared in all its pristine white-and-gray-trimmed beauty.

A flagstone walkway almost perfectly matched the color of the trim, and it was bordered by greenery that, although presently dormant, would burst forth with colorful blossoms in the spring. On either side of the walkway grew an emerald green carpet of grass, and beneath two large front bay windows stood window boxes filled with more shiny-leaved plants.

"Oh, Donovan, it's beautiful."

Her awed whisper caused him to bristle with pride as he followed her up the single step that led to a small open porch. He fitted his key into the lock after sparing her a smile. "I'm glad you approve," he said softly. "Originally this was a two-bedroom, one-bath cottage like the others on the estate. I was able to save most of the framework, which saved me a bundle when I added the extra rooms."

Her eyes were round with surprise as she followed him inside, her admiring gaze encompassing the small tiled foyer and the surrounding living room area. "You did all this yourself?"

"Most of it, although I had a little help from T.J. and Paco and some of the other boys who are interested in learning to build. Carpentry is a hobby of mine, but I'm lousy at wiring and plumbing. I hired independent contractors for those jobs, but the rest was strictly my dream child. The renovation took nearly a year, but I was almost sorry when it was finished. Pounding nails is an excellent way to ease a man's tension and get his creative juices flowing.

"Come on, slowpoke." With a hand at the small of her back, he urged her toward a hallway on their left. "I'll give you a tour while we wait for our dinner to arrive. I told them not to deliver it until seven o'clock, so we have a few minutes left."

Donovan's hand lingered, sliding from her back to circle her shoulders as he showed her his home. She had changed into a sleeveless, full-skirted sundress patterned with multihued flowers, and she was overly conscious of the warmth of his palm against her bare flesh. His touch was like a brand, its heat searing a message of arousal through her brain and into every inch of her body.

When his hip brushed against hers as they passed through a doorway, she shivered, and he turned concerned eyes in her direction. "Are you cold?"

Avoiding his eyes, she managed a negative shake of her head with credible calm. "I'm fine."

Donovan seemed satisfied with her reply, but she wasn't at all pleased with the direction her thoughts seemed to be taking. The yearning she was experiencing, a need to be held in his arms until all her doubts and fears regarding the future slipped away, was growing stronger with every moment that passed. Whether it was right or wrong, she wanted this man with a desperation that was frightening in its intensity.

Frantically seeking a distraction that would lessen the effect of his presence, she allowed her glance to encompass her surroundings. As she did so, she discovered yet another facet of Donovan's complex personality. All of the rooms they passed through were light and airy, with large windows, and skylights set into the ceilings. The white walls should have given an effect of cold formality, but he had managed to retain a cozy, welcoming atmosphere by preserving the cottage's original wooden ceiling beams. The luxurious wall-to-wall carpeting installed throughout was creamy gold pile that complemented the earth-toned furnishings and the desert-themed paintings on the walls.

His home was like him, she decided with quiet admiration. Beautifully formed, solid and unpretentious, with an underlying strength that promised a safe harbor in the midst of any turmoil. But even as the idea formed in her mind, Shannon found herself debating its accuracy. This was Donovan's sanctuary—not hers. Less than four days from now, she would be leaving; she had to remember that. For her, these surroundings, as well as the man who had created them, could never be more than a temporary haven.

Although the thought brought with it a crushing sadness, she sternly repressed the depression that followed in its wake. She was going to enjoy every moment she had with this man, she vowed silently, and the devil take tomorrow. She had spent all of her life being cautious and sensible, and she was sick and tired of taking the safe road through life. The only things those estimable characteristics had ever earned her was loneliness and the certainty that she had missed something vital to her happiness on her climb toward maturity.

Now she was a grown woman, with the self-control needed to confront her own sensuality, and with the intelligence to maintain her autonomy while doing so. The desire she felt for Donovan had become another facet of her feminine psyche, and she had no intention of denying herself by fighting against what she felt for him. He had become vitally important to her, and she wasn't going to negate what she felt by letting caution override her emotions.

Her decision made her feel as if a weight had been lifted from her shoulders, and she preceded Donovan into his library with a new spring in her step. The room was a quiet oasis of serenity, complete with oak shelves and a small quarried-stone fireplace. But the game room was more suited to her buoyant mood this evening. It boasted a pool table, a monstrous wide-screen television, and a wet bar that, she noticed upon further inspection, stocked nonalcoholic beverages. Obviously Donovan wasn't much of a drinker, and he wouldn't want to encourage his kids to be, either.

They had just reached a pair of carved double doors at the end of the hallway when the sound of chimes interrupted their progress. "There's the delivery boy with our dinner. You go on in and take a look around while I get the door, Shannon."

Tiny frown lines appeared between her brows as she watched him leave, and she reluctantly turned to face the entrance to the only room she had yet to inspect. She had been shown several guest rooms, all beautifully decorated and unoccupied. This, then, must be the master bedroom, she thought nervously, her hand trembling slightly as she reached out and grasped two matching wrought-iron handles.

Shannon's knees felt weak as she hesitantly entered the room. Her attention was immediately caught by one item of furniture, and one item only. Minutes passed in silence as she stared down at a king-size bed covered with a soft brown fur spread. Her breathing was rushed and uneven, and she was afraid her heart was going to burst. She was certain of it when Donovan's voice drawled, "I like a lot of space."

Hanging on to her composure by a thread, she glanced over her shoulder and eyed his tall form with a strained smile. "I think in your case a bed this big could be considered a necessity, not an indulgence."

Her mouth went dry when he strolled across the room, a sensuous gleam in his eyes. Cupping her shoulders in a gentle clasp, he urged her closer to his warm, vibrant body. His sweetly scented breath wafted across her face, and she licked her lips to try to capture the taste of him. Her senses were alive as never before, and she knew her face must be expressing a mingling of excitement and hesitation.

Donovan's eyes darkened as he studied her mouth, and when he spoke, his voice was a gravelly whisper that sent shivers dancing along her spine. "I've never brought a woman here, but there's plenty of room for two, Shannon."

"Donovan..." His name was a faint protest; the words that followed were a barely audible reminder. "I thought we weren't going to have an affair. Are you sure this is what you want?"

"I'm sure if you are."

She was certain, because she cared for him, but that knowledge didn't reassure her as it should have. Donovan had no idea that her feelings for him had deepened to the extent that they had, and by failing to tell him of the love she was beginning to feel, she was being deceptive. Once again she glanced toward his bed, and swallowed with difficulty. Loving him meant she wasn't exactly playing by the rules, she acknowledged guiltily, quickly averting her eyes from his too-perceptive gaze.

With a laugh that held more than a trace of panic, she stepped back and tried to lighten the tension that had risen between them at her failure to answer his question. "I thought you were starving...."

He studied her mouth as though he was dying to have it beneath his. "I'm ravenous."

Tilting her head to one side, she studied him with a smile. "Abstinence can be good for the waistline."

His face remained rigid, not a trace of humor softening his features. "Right now my appetite is directed a little farther south, honey."

Shannon gasped at his audacious remark, and a giggle escaped her parted lips. "Somehow I don't think you have food on your mind, Mr. Lancaster."

"How did you guess, Ms. Dalton?"

Donovan's heated glance paused at the dimple in her cheek, and his hand rose to caress the tiny indentation. Instantly he was flooded with a sensation of tenderness. He felt as if every molecule in his body were stretching, expanding, to encompass a joyful elation he had never experienced before. She was a new sun in his sky, bringing warmth to the cold places in his soul. She was light in his darkness, and a melody in a heart that had been too long without the solace of music. She was Shannon, and he was shaken by the realization of how much she already meant to him.

She observed the withdrawal in his eyes, frowning with concern. "What's wrong, Donovan?"

Her intuitiveness caused him to experience a swift stab of resentment that he sought to hide, along with the strain he was feeling. "What could be wrong?" he asked with forced jocularity. "You and me, alone here in my bedroom, is a dream come true for me."

Studying his tense features, she murmured, "Is it?" He began rubbing his thumb over her cheek, but Shannon refused to be diverted. "Please don't be evasive with me, Donovan. I know something's bothering you, but I can't decide whether to back off or try to get you to open up to me. Since I've never learned the rules governing an affair, I would appreciate a little help about now.''

"That's why my conscience is giving me hell." His fingers speared into the soft curls at her temple, his expression conveying a painful degree of self-disgust. "Your lack of experience shames me, Shannon. I wish I could match your innocence, but I can't turn back the clock and live my life over again."

This time her smile held a sadness she didn't try to conceal. "I rather figured that out for myself during the past few days."

"I'm sorry for avoiding you. I guess I just needed a little time to think things through." His lips twisted wryly. "Since all I managed to think about was how much I wanted you, it was a useless exercise."

"And I've spent the time doing a bit of soul-searching of my own."

His entire body tensed as he asked, "What have you decided?"

"I never thought I'd say this to any man, but I want whatever you're able to give me." She hesitated a moment, then added, "For however long it lasts."

Her honesty caused his heart to pound against the wall of his chest. It was all there in her eyes, he realized, his breath suspended in his throat. The desire, the longing, and that other, devastatingly tender emotion he had seen so many times before when she looked at him. Moved beyond bearing, he whispered, "If you knew what was good for you, you'd take off running right about now."

Once again his concern for her overshadowed his own needs, and any doubts Shannon had about sharing this big bed with Donovan disappeared. She wanted to give him all the love stored in her lonely heart, even if she could never speak the words aloud. She wanted to go to him with unselfish motives, and gather a few precious memories to take with her when her time with him was over.

Her eyes glowing with the tenderness in her heart, she cradled his strong jaw in the palm of her hand. "I don't need to run," she murmured softly. "You are very, very good for me, Mr. Lancaster."

When he would have spoken, she placed a finger against his lips. Her eyes were filled with conviction as she said, "When I'm with you, nothing else seems to matter, and when I'm not, you're all I think about. You make me feel beautiful, and more alive than I've ever been before, Donovan. I want—no, I need—to explore these feelings with you, and I promise I won't ever regret a moment of our time together."

He closed his eyes on a surge of emotion, and his fingers trembled against the soft skin of her cheeks. "I'm trying to be noble, dammit!"

With a husky chuckle, she pressed her hands to the backs of his, delighting in the warmth of his flesh against her face. "Don't strain yourself, noble knight."

His lashes lifted to reveal a new certainty in his troubled gaze. "I wish I could give you everything you deserve, honey."

"What is it you think I deserve?" she asked gently.

With a scowl, he turned and rubbed at the knotted muscles in the back of his neck. Walking over to the window, he stood silently for a long moment, his arms crossed over his chest, his back rigid with tension. He seemed to be gathering his thoughts. "Forever," he finally ground out hoarsely. "You deserve forever, Shannon."

She crossed the room to join him, but paused a few steps away from him. "No one can guarantee forever, Donovan."

He turned suddenly and leaned back against the window casing. Gazing down at her from his superior height, he said, "I know that better than anyone, but you're evading the real issue between us."

"And that is?"

"A relationship with some hope of a future, for pity's sake! Most men could give you a sincere commitment, but I can't."

"Can't or won't, Donovan?"

He hardened himself against the appeal in those gentle emerald eyes, and his chest rose on a harshly drawn breath. How long would it take before her involvement with him stole all that shining innocence from her? he wondered in despair. The laugh he uttered then was a travesty of the real thing, a cynical burst of sound that sliced into Shannon and left her torn and bleeding inside. "I won't," he admitted curtly.

She had to bite down hard on her lower lip to stop its trembling, but when she spoke, her voice was steady. "Because you don't believe in forever?"

With her he could believe in anything, but for her sake all he could offer her was a lie. His eyes as hard as the bones that sculpted his face, he said, "That's part of it, certainly."

Shannon decided that now wasn't the time to hold anything back. Taking a deep breath, she gazed at him challengingly. "Then you're hiding from the truth, Donovan."

"What truth?" he questioned defensively.

"I think you've had too little love in your life for you to believe in your own ability to respond to it, or in anyone else's ability to give it. You don't trust yourself, and you certainly don't trust me."

Tormented by the anguish in her voice, he knew he couldn't let her think that his feelings for her were so shallow. "Trust does come hard for me, but not where you're concerned, Shannon. Integrity shines from you like a beacon, and I was drawn by that quality in you from the moment we met. I guess that's why I acted like such a surly bastard. You threw me off-balance, and I didn't like the idea of being vulnerable."

"Oh!" she gasped, tears filling her eyes. "You don't know how much your trust means to me, Donovan."

He gripped her shoulders and shook her lightly. "It doesn't make any difference, don't you understand? You were right about me. What I feel for you is outside my experience, and as such, it can't be counted on, honey. Life has a way of screwing up the best-laid plans, and I can't stand the thought that I might hurt you someday."

Her chest rose sharply, and a single tear slipped from the corner of her eye. "I understand that you're scared of what's happening between us. So am I. Emotions this strong are frightening, but we can't go on denying ourselves."

"Emotions are as insubstantial and as changeable as the wind, and with just as much potential for destruction, Shannon." His gaze darkened with bitter memories from his past. "Believe me, I know what I'm talking about."

"Yet the wind can also be counted on to exist in one form or another. Whether that existence reflects itself in a gentle breeze or a hurricane, it maintains a constant impact on our lives. We can survive with only oxygen to sustain us, but think of the sweetness that would be lost without the wind to catch at our breath. Emotions are usually no more visible than the wind, but does that mean they're any less real?"

"Oh, they're real enough when we're caught up in the maelstrom," he uttered with a derisive laugh. "But what about later? What happens when that first sweet rush fades into calm, and the real world intrudes on the fantasy?"

"Then we should savor the peace, and be strengthened by the memory of the storm."

He desperately wanted that soft, soothing voice to convince him that his desire for her was right and good, but he knew he would be taking without offering her anything substantial in return. He was ready to rail at her for her obstinate inability to face their incompatibility, when her next words sliced through him with devastating force. "I want to make memories with you, Donovan."

His body shuddered in response, and his tightening hands both held her away and conveyed the possessiveness he felt toward her. "I may not believe that what we feel for each other will last longer than a day, a week, a month, but heaven help me, I can't hold out much longer against you. If you don't get out of here right now, I'll take everything you have to give and say to hell with the consequences."

Shannon began to release the few remaining buttons on his shirt, leaning forward to place a kiss against the hollow of his throat. "Then take me, Donovan."

His hands speared into her hair, and he tilted her head back until her eyes collided with his narrow-lidded gaze. "You'd better be damned sure this is what you want," he warned her through gritted teeth. "Another few minutes of having you rub up against me, and you'll no longer have a choice."

With deliberate provocativeness, she brushed her upper torso from side to side, her nipples tightening to pebble-hardness as they pressed against his muscular frame. A teasing smile curved her lips. "Like this, darling?"

Whether it was the endearment or the feel of her small, rounded breasts, with their pointed nipples, burrowing into his chest, Donovan's resistance faded into nothingness in that instant. With a groan of arousal, he lowered his head, and slanted his lips over hers. His mouth moved back and forth with hungry urgency, but Shannon didn't need to be coaxed into opening for his invasion. She was rewarded by the bold, searching sweep of his tongue, and a low moan revealed the extent of her pleasure.

Eagerly she slid her arms over his shoulders, and cradled his nape with her hands. Donovan reacted with a sharp intake of breath, his own arms winding around her waist as he pulled her body high and hard against his own. Due to the disparity in their heights, she was nearly lifted off her feet, since he wasn't satisfied until her soft femininity cradled his straining sex through their clothing.

They were trembling uncontrollably by the time he ended the kiss, but an ingrained sense of responsibility had him pulling his head back with a jerk. He was taking enough chances with Shannon's future happiness, he realized grimly, without landing her with a baby she hadn't planned. His features strained from the effort it was costing him to control the desire burning in him, he gasped, "Shannon, I didn't plan for this to happen tonight. I'm not prepared, honey. I haven't slept with a woman in a very long time, so there's been no reason to keep myself supplied with protection. Unless you're on the pill, our lovemaking poses something of a problem."

Shannon would have given anything to avoid the next few minutes, and every muscle in her body clenched in dread anticipation. Except for her cousin Debra and her ex-fiancé, no one had been told the secret she had carried for so many years. Donovan's concern for her well-being had earned him the right to be told the truth, but getting the words past the tense blockage in her throat proved an impossibility.

She opened her mouth, and a strangled sound emerged. When he drew back to look at her, his expression registered shock at how pale she had become. "What is it, honey?"

Her eyes filling with tears, she lowered her gaze to the middle of his chest. With a blunt honesty that ripped her apart inside, she whispered, "I can't have children, Donovan."

His sharp inhalation of breath was the only sound in the room. She wanted to scream at him to say something, to put her out of her misery. Several seconds passed, and her agony increased a thousandfold. His hesitation reinforced her certainty of rejection, and by the time he told her how sorry he was she was already struggling to free herself. With a muffled sob, she pushed her hands against his chest, and the tears she had been suppressing trickled through the barrier of her closed eyelids. "Let me go!" she cried.

"Not a chance." He drew her closer and rested his cheek against the silky softness of her hair. "Talk to me, sweetheart."

With a despairing moan, she sagged against him, and as if a dam had broken, words began to flow from her mouth. She told him of the doctor's verdict that had shattered her hopes and killed her dreams, and of her fiancé's defection. She talked until she was too spent and drained to utter another sound. In a voice filled with disgust, Donovan muttered, "If I had your old boyfriend here, I'd wring his neck like a chicken."

Shannon giggled, well able to imagine Frank's skinny neck flopping back and forth as Donovan strangled him. Then she sniffled, and self-consciously swiped at the tears staining her face. "Have you got a handkerchief I could borrow?"

Donovan grinned when she wiped the back of her hand against her nose like a child, and reached into the top drawer of a nearby bureau. Handing her a folded white square, he asked, "Feel better now?"

"Oddly enough, I do."

"It's not odd at all." Bending his head, he pressed a gentle kiss against her mouth. "You've been holding the pain inside you for too long, honey. It's about time you let it out."

Shannon's hands returned to his chest. Her gaze was locked on them as she twisted the handkerchief between her fingers. Taking a deep breath, she asked hesitantly, "Do you still want me?"

Gently he took the handkerchief away from her, dropped it on the floor and lifted both her hands to his mouth. With a tenderness that hurt him as much as the pain she had shared with him, he rasped, "More than ever."

With a laugh that nearly deteriorated into another sob, she searched his features with glistening, adoring eyes.

'Then make me your lover, because it's what I want more than anything else in the world, Donovan.''

He closed his eyes on a surge of emotion, and pressed his lips against her forehead. ''Then let's make our first memory together.''

Bending to lift her in his arms, he whispered hoarsely, 'Let's create the sweetest memory any lovers ever have.''

Donovan carried her toward the bed and stood her on her feet. Shannon felt explosive tremors shaking her as he began to remove her clothing, his mouth and hands caressing each inch of flesh he exposed to his gaze. A fire burned hot inside her, and this time the tears that trickled down her cheeks expressed so much joy that she wanted to shout her happiness to the world.

He murmured unintelligibly as he stood her on her feet and began kissing the tears away from her soft skin, tearing at his own clothes as he did so. Only when they were both naked and equally vulnerable did he allow his eyes to wander over her body. ''Dear heaven, you're as beautiful and perfect as I remembered, sweetheart.''

His words made her ache for a more tactile expression of approval. ''Touch me,'' she moaned. ''Please...don't make me wait any longer, Donovan.''

Once again he lifted her into his arms and laid her in the middle of the large bed. He didn't bother to pull back the fur spread. He wanted to enjoy the erotic contrast of white skin and flaming hair against a sea of brown, and he paused with one knee poised on the mattress beside her lissome body. The bed nearly swallowed her tiny form, and an amused grin curved his mouth.

''So small and sweet,'' he murmured as his lips sought out her delicate features, ''and yet every inch a woman.''

Her hands reached up, and she burrowed her fingers in the crisp, curling hair spread so thickly over his chest. ''Of the two of us, you're the more beautiful,'' she said, sighing complacently.

Laughter shook his body, but then, suddenly, he stilled, and his eyes caught fire. Slowly positioning himself over her until they were melded together from breast to thigh, he braced his arms beside her head and moaned in satisfaction. She buried her face in the hollow of his throat, and her lips vibrated with his gasping breaths. Her own breathing quickened, and she began to move against him in an unconscious rhythm. Her nipples tightened almost painfully as they came into contact with the abrasive pelt of hair covering his muscular chest, and she cried out in response.

The sound sent sinuous ripples of pleasure over his moistening flesh, and he began a gentle rocking motion against her. "Is this what you like, baby?"

Another whimper burst from her throat, and she arched her back to deepen the teasing contact. "I'm on fire, Donovan."

"That's what I want you to do, little flame," he murmured huskily. "I want you to burn in my arms, and devour me in the inferno."

As though he couldn't wait another moment, he captured her mouth with hungry urgency. His kiss was passionate, masterful, his need for her fiercely demanding. But Shannon's need was no less urgent, and she opened her lips eagerly to the sweet, devouring sweep of his tongue. He tasted and savored the honeyed depths of her mouth for what seemed like an eternity, and by the time he lifted his head she was writhing against him in mind-spinning ecstasy.

"Slowly, sweetheart..." Gritting his teeth as he fought for control, he muttered, "Let's take this slow and easy, or I just might finish before you get started."

Shannon, too, gritted her teeth, and her eyes were wild as she looked up at him. "I can't wait any longer, Donovan. Please... I can't!"

"You can, my flame." This time the kiss he pressed against her lips was lazily affectionate. "I want to take the ime to savor the magic, sweet Shannon. I need to imprint ou on my senses so thoroughly that you'll always be a part f me.''

She drew his head down to hers and spoke against his mouth. "A part of each other, Donovan.''

He kissed her hungrily for several minutes before lowering his head to her breasts, which by now were throbbing with need for the touch of his mouth. At the teasing brush f his tongue against one aching, distended nipple, she rched her back and silently offered herself to him. Donovan didn't need further encouragement. With a low, growling murmur, he enveloped the shimmering bud with his lips, nd began a gentle suckling that had Shannon's hips rising nd falling in voluptuous abandon.

Donovan continued working his magic on her until she ecame a shivering, groaning mass of need. Their mouths net once more, and this time the kiss was hot enough to onsume them both. Jerking her head back on a gasp, she leaded, "Donovan, I need . . . I need . . .''

He knew what she needed, and he shared her urgency. wiftly he slid his hand from her breast to the satiny flesh of er thigh. "Open for me, sweetheart.''

Shannon did as he asked, and was rewarded by a light, robing touch of his fingers against the portals of her yomanhood. As he fondled her ever deeper, his mouth reurned to her breasts. As the movements of his hand beame bolder, he nibbled and licked and suckled her nipples. Iis head moved from one plump mound to the other, the newling cries of pleasure she uttered nearly driving him over he edge.

It was Shannon who was first propelled into a swirling naelstrom by the sorcerer's touch, her shivering becoming convulsive release so intense she nearly fainted. She had ever experienced anything like the climax that lifted her up nd flung her into spinning ecstasy. Over and over again she ried out Donovan's name, and her voice was raw and rasping by the time the final ripples of sensation faded away into a peaceful nirvana.

But Donovan's moment had come, and he eagerly positioned himself between her thighs. "Open your eyes and look at me, Shannon."

She did as he asked, and gasped as the tip of his manhood began to penetrate the passion-moistened depths of her body. But Donovan found it impossible to sustain her gaze for very long, and his lashes fluttering downward as his most treasured fantasy was realized. Darkness only intensified the exquisite sensation of becoming a part of Shannon, and he didn't know how much longer he could hold back his own release.

His trembling arms barely able to hold his weight, he stiffened above her. "Don't move, baby," he gasped through gritted teeth. "Please . . . don't . . . move. . . ."

"Oh, Donovan..." She sighed, lost in the beauty of their joining.

Carefully, in achingly slow increments, he pushed his hips forward until he filled her completely. Shannon felt a small measure of discomfort at first, his thick hardness almost more than she could take. But soon her body had stretched to accommodate him, and each careful stroke of his manhood led her deeper into a joy so great she thought she could die happily in that instant.

Donovan climaxed with her, his head thrown back and a triumphant cry bursting from his parted lips. He felt as if he had been ripped apart and put back together again, a stronger, more complete version of the man he had been before. Before Shannon. Before warmth and joy. He collapsed with a groan of soul-deep satisfaction, and surrendered completely to the arms that held him so tightly.

Eight

Donovan rolled onto his side, taking Shannon with him. Cradling her in the crook of his arm, he kissed the damp curls at her temple. "I never knew, Shannon."

Tilting her head back, she gazed up at him with drowsy, questioning eyes. With a smile he felt all the way through his body, he whispered, "I never knew lovemaking could be like that, so... so complete."

Shannon's expression reflected her surprise and delight. "Shouldn't that be my line?"

"You tell me," he suggested, a mocking slant to one eyebrow. "Should it?"

She lifted her head, and the eyes that met his sparkled with a joyousness that caught at his breath. "You know, it's strange, Donovan. I loved my fiancé, but after last night I realize the limitations there were in our relationship.

"He never really reached me completely. At the time, I was too inexperienced to sense that there was anything lacking, but he must have been aware of the physical and emotional chasms between us. Maybe that's why he strayed, and not, as I'd always assumed, because I couldn't give him children.''

"That doesn't excuse his behavior," Donovan ground out harshly. "A man should honor his commitments."

"He did honor one commitment," she reminded him wryly. "He married the woman who was pregnant with his child."

"The bastard should have stood by you."

Although the words were uttered fiercely, the hand that brushed a stray tendril of hair from her cheek was exquisitely gentle. His eyes were eloquent with emotion, and his tender concern for the pain she had suffered in the past brought a lump to her throat. With trembling fingers, she traced the curve of his jaw and whispered, "You've made me feel like a whole woman again, Donovan."

He quickly clasped her face between his hands, and his eyes darkened with intensity. "Listen up, and listen good," he said curtly. "A woman's femininity isn't dependent upon her child-bearing capacity, Shannon."

"But a man wants—"

"Neither should a man's masculinity be based upon his ability to father children," he told her forcefully, interrupting her. "Two people become parents through loving and growing and understanding their children, not because they gave life to them. You would make a wonderful mother because you are a wonderful woman, and God knows there are an awful lot of homeless kids in the world who would agree with me."

His words began to heal a wound that had festered for too long inside her, and with a sigh of relief she reclined until her entire body was snuggled against his length. When his arm obligingly reached out to keep her anchored firmly to his side, her head found a blissfully comfortable hollow between his neck and shoulder. "Thank you," she murmured softly.

She looked up in time to see his mouth curve into a contented smile. "I assure you, the pleasure was all mine, honey."

She contradicted him, with a smile of her own. "Not all." As she searched his eyes, her expression was alight with a kind of awestruck happiness. "Becoming a part of you was like dying and experiencing a rebirth, Donovan."

Her confession so closely matched his earlier thoughts that he was stunned into silence. Their gazes held for long, endless moments, as each of them savored an inner communion that went beyond anything language could convey. Then he shifted on his side until he faced her. One arm still cradled her shoulders, but his other hand was busy languidly stroking the smooth curve of her spine.

"You and I together could light up the world." He sighed. "Physically we are one hell of an explosive combination, and right now every bone in my body seems to have turned to mush. Yet lying here beside you, I feel strong enough to push the moon out of orbit."

He used some of that strength to squeeze the resilient flesh of her buttocks. "I don't know if you realize it," he growled drowsily, "but you have a delightfully sexy tush."

She gave a mewl of pleasure and started her own journey of exploration. As her fingers slid over his shoulder and down his chest, she grinned impishly. "Yours isn't bad, either, but I prefer the frontal approach."

When she reached his stomach, he stiffened and muttered a warning. "You're invading dangerous territory, woman."

"I'm not worried." She slipped her hand lower, and when he gasped, her giggle held a trace of smugness. "Poor baby, you're all worn out."

"You think so?" With a suddenness that brought a startled cry to her lips, he rose up on the elbow that cradled her head. As he studied her delicately sculpted features, his lids narrowed over eyes that blazed with emotion.

"Donovan?" she questioned uncertainly.

Almost reflexively, his arm formed a tighter curve around her shoulders. He bent to press a brief kiss to the arched column of her throat, and his parted lips felt the vibration of the breath she drew into her lungs. Her pulse was beating strongly, and he paused to savor the reality of her life force with a caressing tongue before slowly lifting his head.

Cupping her smooth, rounded chin in his hand, he held her gaze and whispered, "I want you again."

"Mmm . . ." she murmured in agreement.

Her hands rose to begin gently exploring his strong, decisive features with the tips of her fingers. Her touch was feather-light against the subtle arch of his dark brows, and she smiled as she felt the tiny creases in his forehead deepen as his eyelids drifted closed. Taking advantage of the opportunity he had just given her, she brushed the pads of her fingers over his feathery lashes.

With teasing petulance, she murmured a complaint. "It's no fair."

Without opening his eyes, he asked, "What isn't fair?"

"For you to have lashes this long and thick."

Although his eyes remained closed, the lashes in question flickered as his lips quirked with devilish intent. "I can think of another area where those qualities didn't displease you."

Shannon uttered a strangled gasp, but then her laughter rang out. "Donovan Lancaster, you are a wicked, wicked man."

"And you are the sexiest woman I've ever tangled with."

"Will you stop teasing me?"

His eyelids rose, and she was instantly captured in a sensual aura that made her quiver with awareness. His voice a dark honey promise, he muttered, "Who's teasing?"

With a swiftness that left her mind spinning along with her body, he flopped onto his back and lifted her until she was sprawled on top of him. Chuckling at the squeal that burst from her throat, he smoothed his hands over the taut skin at her waist. When he reached her hips, his fingers paused to test the rounded fullness of the burgeoning flesh.

"Still think I'm teasing?" he drawled as he altered her position slightly.

Bracing her arms against his broad chest for leverage, she reared back and gaped at him in surprise. "What do you think you are, some kind of iron man?"

Blazingly white teeth flashed in a grin sensual enough to short-circuit her nerve endings. He murmured words of praise and encouragement as he drew her knees forward and levered her upper body into a sitting position. Once she was straddling him to his satisfaction, he raised his head to give his mouth access to her breasts. He left strings of kisses over every inch of the sweetly curved mounds, before opening his mouth over first one peaking nipple and then the other.

Throwing her head back, Shannon closed her eyes as sharp darts of pleasure speared through her body. But Donovan was after a fuller expression of her passion, and his fingers continued to glide sinuously up her silky-soft thighs. Reaching his goal, he gently parted the swollen, petal-soft folds of her womanhood with his thumbs. "So you don't think I'm capable, hmm? Wanna bet?"

As he entered her with a driving thrust that nearly stopped her heart, she decided that now was definitely no time to begin an argument.

Shannon awakened slowly from one of the most blissful, restful sleeps she had ever experienced. She didn't know what it was that had pulled her from the depths of slumber, until her ears became attuned to her conscious state. Almost immediately the sound came again, this time louder and more insistent. Her eyes remained closed, but a grin twitched the corners of her lips as she realized that she was listening to Donovan's stomach growling.

They had completely forgotten about the dinner that awaited them in the kitchen, she recalled, both of them too concerned with satisfying other hungers to remember much of anything. She was surprised that Donovan's protesting stomach hadn't already roused him, but she could tell from the even tenor of his breathing that he was still asleep. Good, she thought with drowsy contentment.

Tightening her arm around his waist, she cuddled closer against his side. She wasn't ready to get up yet. His fur-nacelike warmth was too seductive not to be enjoyed to the fullest. Rubbing her cheek against his furry chest with all the satisfaction of a feline basking in the sun, she replayed in her mind the hours just spent in his arms with lazy content-ment.

Although she wanted to remain lost in her thoughts, she gradually became aware of the passage of time. With a re-luctant sigh, she carefully lifted the covers Donovan had draped over them before they fell asleep. Once free of the confining bedding, she slowly raised herself up on her el-bow and glanced over him at the luminous hands of the clock radio on his nightstand. She was relieved to discover that it was only a little after eleven.

Rolling over as quietly as possible, so that she wouldn't wake him, she scooted to the edge of the bed and began to lower her feet to the floor. But before she could stand, a re-straining hand at her waist jerked her backward, and a husky voice growled a question against the nape of her neck. "Where do you think you're going?"

Before she had a chance to reply, Donovan pulled her over on top of him. She gazed down at his tousled hair and his sleep-dazed eyes, and failed to summon up even a smidgen of indignation. "It's getting late," she whispered, gently brushing the tangled locks away from his frown-wrinkled forehead. "I need to get to bed."

"Mmm..." he murmured, glancing at the breast brush-ing against his chest with masculine appreciation. "Unless

I'm having a wonderfully erotic dream, you're already in bed.''

"My own bed," she told him firmly, attempting to lever herself off him. "Curfew is at midnight, Donovan."

Her straining arms proved ineffectual against the strength of his. "Spend the night with me."

Pressing a kiss against his chin, she shook her head regretfully. "You know I can't do that."

"Why in hell not?"

Shannon grinned at his grouchy disappointment, but stood firm in her decision. "Rules are not made to be broken, and..."

His tongue began to trace the dimple in her cheek, and she forgot what she'd been about to say. But Donovan successfully filled in the blanks. "And I'm the damn fool who thought up the idea of a curfew in the first place."

Sitting up, she gave his arm a consoling pat. "You go back to sleep. I can see myself home."

He glared at her, threw back the covers and bounded to his feet with an energy she envied. "You're not walking back to the shelter alone."

"There's nearly a full moon out tonight and the path is well lit."

"Nor are you leaving here without eating dinner," he insisted in a no-nonsense tone of voice. "If you want to take a quick shower while I heat the food in the microwave, you'll find towels in the cabinet under the sink."

"But I'm really not hungry, and I—"

"Don't argue."

With an air of distraction, he began to search the floor for his discarded clothing. "If you get any smaller, I'll have to shake the sheets to find you."

Although she collected her own clothing from the floor, Shannon was too busy watching Donovan to bother getting dressed. Instead, she stood in silent fascination, her sweeping glance taking in the perfection of his splendid physique. The faint light filtering through the window gilded him with moonglow, and her mouth went dry as she visually inspected the body she now knew so well by touch.

Moistening her lips with the tip of her tongue, she watched as he decided to forgo his shorts and slid his jeans over his lean hips. The hiss of the zipper sounded as loud as the blood pounding in her head, and her heart took off at an incredible clip when he sucked in his flat, hair-dusted stomach to fasten the snap at his waist. He was hairy all over, from his collarbone to his ankles, and she trembled as she remembered how all that fur-covered flesh had felt against her naked body.

"Keep looking at me like that," a deep voice warned her, "and we'll never get out of here."

Shannon lifted her head in a hurry, but couldn't do anything to prevent the heated blush that stained her cheeks. When he grinned in amusement, she spun around with an embarrassed murmur of exasperation. There was a haughty tilt to her chin as she passed him, but she completely spoiled the regal effect by glaring at him over her shoulder. "You have a perverted sense of humor, Mr. Lancaster!"

There was a leering gleam in his eyes as he thoroughly inspected the lush nakedness of her backside. "Indubitably, Ms. Dalton."

With a disdainful sniff, she slammed the bathroom door shut with a backward kick, and gasped at the pain that speared upward from her heel. Dropping her clothes on the floor, she muttered dire predictions as to the fate of the laughing jackass in the other room. But as she knelt down to rub her bruised foot, there was the tiniest hint of a smile on her face.

By the time her last evening at Lancaster House arrived, Shannon didn't have any smiles left. Somehow she got through the farewell party the kids had planned for her without bursting into tears, but during the hours that folowed her composure began to crack into little pieces, along with her heart. She and Donovan spent their last hours together wrapped in each other's arms in front of the fireplace in the library, while she silently prayed for him to ask her to stay. He remained silent.

Up until then, she had convinced herself that she was prepared for their parting. Her departure plans were made, she and her cousin and Tricia had said their goodbyes at the party, and most of her clothing was packed. All the practical aspects of leaving had been accomplished with her usual competence, but inside she was dying at the thought of being separated from this man she now admitted she loved with every fiber of her being. She clung to him in desperation, and ached to plead with him to change his mind. But she remained silent.

When Donovan left her at the rear entrance to Lancaster House, one final, lingering kiss challenged the last of her courage. With a muffled sob, she tore herself free of his embrace, and rushed inside the building before scalding, pain-racked tears began to bleed from her burning eyes. As she leaned her forehead against the closed door, another sob ripped her apart, and she allowed the agonizing pain to have its way. It was then that she realized she had lied to Donovan when she promised him there would be no regrets.

Donovan was staring sightlessly out the window of his study when the phone beside him began to ring. His entire body tensed at the sound, and a black scowl disturbed the evenness of his features. He knew who was on the other end of the line, and he had been alternately expecting and dreading this moment. Shannon had chosen to drive back to Los Angeles, and last night she had promised to call him when she was ready to be taken to pick up the rental car she had ordered.

Last night, after they had made love for the last time! The thought disturbed him far more than the jarring buzz of the telephone, but all his suppressed aggression was centered in the hand that jerked the receiver from its cradle. His first name was bitten out in staccato syllables, as though that, too, offended him. As he listened to the brief message, which was given in a voice so strained it was barely intelligible, he closed his eyes as pain ripped through him in a vicious tide.

But all he said was "I'll bring the car around to the front entrance, Shannon. Tell Sam and T.J. to meet me there with your luggage."

After he hung up the phone, his eyes returned to the view outside. The sky was overcast, and the air was heavy with the promise of rain. The trees along the perimeter of his property were almost completely bare, and wind-tossed brown leaves liberally littered the ground around their sturdy trunks. The last of the Indian-summer weather they had so briefly enjoyed had given way to nature's preparations for winter, and it would be spring before new growth returned to those barren limbs.

Donovan's hands clenched into fists at his sides as he wondered where Shannon would be in the spring. She wouldn't return here—that he knew for certain. He had known it last night, from the frenzied desperation of their lovemaking. He had known it when he kissed her goodbye at the shelter and felt the trembling of her lips beneath his own. He had known it when he looked into her eyes and viewed the tears she wouldn't allow to fall.

Most of all, he had known it when she pulled free of his encircling arms and the wind carried her muffled sobs back to him. He had stood there and let her go, afraid to call her back. Afraid of what he might do or say. Afraid to acknowledge the extent of his own anguish. Afraid to accept how lost and alone he felt at that moment, or to admit, even to himself, how desperately he needed her to stay with him.

He was still afraid.

With a muttered curse, he spun on his heel, and stormed through the house as though the hounds of hell were chasing him. Everywhere he looked, he saw Shannon, and with a sinking sensation he wondered if her memory would always haunt him. Her touch, her scent, her taste, seemed indelibly imprinted on his mind, as were the images of an impish smile, a pair of bright green eyes, and the fiery curls he loved to run his fingers through.

A moisture-rich wind buffeted him as he strode toward his car. Nature's mood seemed as sullen as his own. Clenching his teeth, he seated himself and twisted the key in the ignition. As he accelerated down the drive, he dreaded reaching his destination. Suddenly feeling stifled, he cracked open the window at his side. The cool breeze that blew through the aperture between door frame and window fanned his face, but brought no relief from his inner torment.

The sound the wind made as it whistled through the gap reminded him too much of Shannon's sweet, melodious trill of laughter. He could picture her at his side, her lovely face alight with mischief as she turned in his direction. So many times she had looked at him in just such a way, her beautiful eyes flooding his heart with warmth and banishing the loneliness from his soul. Then the vision vanished, and he was alone once again. By the time he reached the shelter, his hands were aching from the fierceness of his grip on the steering wheel.

Nine

Shannon refused to cry as she folded the few items of clothing she hadn't already packed and carefully placed them inside her brown leather suitcase. Her overnight bag was already loaded with makeup and toiletries, and early this morning she had given these rooms a thorough cleaning. She hadn't been able to sleep anyway, and she had been glad to have something to occupy her mind and hands. Now all she had to do was zip her case closed, collect her jacket and purse and walk out of the shelter.

That last task was going to be more difficult than anything she had ever done before, she realized, feeling every muscle in her body tighten in revolt. Although she was growing accustomed to the uncomfortable sensation, she wasn't able to keep herself from reacting adversely to the tension coiling inside her. Her palms were moist, her jaw ached from the way she was clenching her teeth, and her head was throbbing.

As a muffled sound penetrated her self-absorption, she glanced jerkily over her shoulder at the solemn faces peering at her from her doorway. The jaunty smile she attempted faltered before it could reach her eyes, and she was unable to withstand the disapproval aimed in her direction. Nervous beneath that silent scrutiny, she began straightening the hem of the thigh-length blue sweater she wore over a snug pair of blue-and-rose flowered leggings.

The movement was calculated more as a means to hide the trembling of her fingers than out of a desire for neatness, and her hands grew still as a tall, lanky young man with brooding dark eyes pressed forward. Avoiding her gaze, he bent down to collect her cases. "I'll take these to the car for you, Shannon."

Her throat tight, she nodded. "Thank you, Sam."

Another, stockier-framed youth followed on Sam's heels. A vivid scar puckered the flesh from his right temple to the corner of his mouth, disturbing the even symmetry of a face otherwise as smooth as polished ebony. Bending to grasp the handle of the last and largest case, he said, "You cook a damn sight better than Linda. The lion's a fool for lettin' you go."

"I appreciate the compliment, T.J., but it's time I returned home," she said gently. "I'll miss you all very much, but don't you worry. I left some of your favorite recipes with Linda, and she promised me she'd use them. Your stomach won't suffer from my absence."

Her attempt at humor fell sadly short of the mark, as both T.J. and Sam gave her swift looks of reproof. "It's not your cooking we're going to miss," Sam countered gruffly.

"You got that right," T.J. agreed, his expression glum. "Some of us guys gave you a pretty hard time when you got here, but you never once ratted on us for bad-mouthing you like we did. You didn't hold no grudge, either. That first night, when you made a big batch of fudge and sat with us in the great room while we scarfed it down, well...you made us feel awful bad, Shannon.''

Deliberately misunderstanding him, her brows rose in teasing arcs. ''My fudge made you sick?''

''You know what I mean!''

This last was uttered in such an aggrieved tone of voice, even the taciturn Sam was forced to smile. ''Do we ever!'' he exclaimed self-righteously. ''By the time you guys headed for your bunks, you were eating more crow than you were fudge.''

T.J. threw him an indignant glare before turning his attention back to Shannon. Holding out his free hand, he muttered, ''No hard feelings?''

Her breath catching in her throat, she placed a trembling hand within his grasp. But she was dissatisfied with the impersonal brevity of the gesture, and she suddenly threw her arms around the sheepishly smiling boy's burly shoulders and kissed his scarred cheek. ''Of course not, hotshot.''

There was a stricken expression in T.J.'s wide brown eyes as he muttered an excuse and quickly bolted out of the room. Sam followed, and as she watched them leave another shape detached itself from the doorway and rushed forward. A pair of thin arms reached out for Shannon and clasped her around the waist with a strength born of desperation. ''I don't want you to go.''

Brushing a hand over the sobbing girl's long dark hair, Shannon barely managed to maintain control over her own emotions. With tears aching for release behind closed eyelids, she whispered, ''It's time for me to leave, Trina. You knew my job here was only temporary.''

''The lion would find something else for you to do if you asked him,'' Trina pleaded. ''You know he would!''

Just another hour, Shannon prayed silently, hugging Trina tightly to her breast. *Dear Lord, please give me the strength to get through one more hour without breaking down.* Swallowing past the lump that had settled in her throat like a boulder, she drew in a slow, calming breath and hoped she could manage to get her vocal chords to function.

"It wouldn't be fair to ask him to manufacture a job for me, now would it?" she questioned softly. "Donovan already has a full staff, honey. He doesn't need me any longer."

Truer words had never been spoken, Shannon decided with anguished certainty. If Donovan needed her half as much as she needed him, he wouldn't be preparing to drive her to pick up the rental car. If he wanted her half as much as she wanted him, he wouldn't be letting her walk out of his life. Damn the man! If he cared for her, even a little, he wouldn't let his fear of commitment stand in his way. So she had to accept the obvious, and face the fact that he didn't care—or at least not enough to take a chance on their relationship.

"But I need you," Trina cried, the edge of fear in her voice successfully wiping Shannon's mind free from her preoccupation with Donovan. "I want you here when the baby's born."

Shannon pressed a kiss upon the head resting against her shoulder, and stared at the far wall without seeing a thing. "I know you do," she said on a quivering inhalation, "and I want to be here. It's just not possible, Trina."

With a shuddering sigh, Trina straightened, and wiped fisted hands over her tear dampened cheeks. "Will you write to me?"

Her voice held the insecurity of a child who had had too many promises broken in her young life, and it took the last remaining shred of willpower Shannon possessed to keep herself from breaking down. "Just try and stop me," she whispered fiercely. "And as soon as the baby's old enough to travel, you and Sam can come visit me."

With the new maturity her pregnancy had brought her, Trina reluctantly gave a negative shake of her head. "We won't be able to afford—''

"You won't have to," Shannon interjected swiftly. "You and Sam decided to forgo a honeymoon to save for the baby, and this trip to L.A. won't cost you a penny. It will be my wedding present to you both, if you don't mind having me along as a third wheel."

Once again Trina threw her arms around Shannon, and her cheek was once again damp with tears as she cried, "I love you!"

"I love you, too, sweetheart."

Shannon watched in numbed misery as Trina tore off down the hallway and disappeared around a corner. Blankly her gaze wandered over an area that was now bare of her personal effects. She knew she would be leaving a large part of herself behind when she walked out of this room. She would be returning to the condominium she had bought and decorated to suit her needs, but she felt no pleasure at the thought of going home. Without the people she loved to share it with her, it was just a sterile dwelling place, bereft of warmth and happiness. Her heart would remain here at the shelter, where she really belonged.

She didn't know why she felt that way—or maybe she did, she amended silently. She was a giver by nature. That facet of her personality she had always accepted and taken for granted. But she was also a woman who was tired of walking an emotional tightrope. Until coming here, she hadn't realized how much love was bottled up inside her, just waiting to be set free.

In that instant, she knew beyond a shadow of a doubt that she wasn't going to return to her job at the hospital. Neonatal nurses couldn't afford to become too personally involved with their charges, or let their effectiveness be weakened by emotion. Nor could they let their decisions be affected by self-interest. Babies lived and were taken home

y their parents, or they died and were taken home by the
Lord. Either way, they were lost to those who had so briefly
become such a vital part of their lives.

Stiffening her spine, she clenched her fists and struggled
with the knowledge that tore at the entire fabric of the life
she had fashioned for herself. Because of Donovan, because of Trina and Sam and T.J. and Paco and all of the
other friends she'd made at the shelter, she wasn't the same
woman who had arrived here such a short time ago, full of
self-doubt and guilt. Now she knew that she had to be open
to love, and chance loss as well as joy if she hoped to achieve
a healthy balance.

When had she allowed ambition to replace dedication?
she asked herself. When had she stopped letting herself feel,
because to do so would be to risk her sanity? Although she
had suppressed the realization, each baby she relinquished
to its parents had taken a little piece of her heart, and each
baby that couldn't be saved had taken a measure of her soul.
Without love from a family of her own to replenish the
losses she was incurring on a daily basis, she had become a
burned-out shell.

She had been functioning like an automaton, without
even the reserves of strength necessary to properly care for
herself. Yes, she needed to have others need her. But she had
needs of her own, needs that had to be met if she was to realize her potential as a fully functioning, intelligent human
being. She desperately needed a return of the affection she
expended, just as much as, or perhaps even more than, she
needed to give that affection to others.

Shannon realized now how much she craved T.J.'s macho protectiveness and Tricia's shy smiles and Sam's taciturn approval. And she needed Donovan. *Oh, Lord, how
she needed Donovan!* She was addicted to the man. She
craved the sound of his voice, and she constantly hungered
for the emptiness inside her to be filled by his hard, demanding body.

And in spite of his failure to allow any true depth to their relationship, that stubbornly proud, suspiciously vulnerable idiot needed her just as much. At the thought, her mouth compressed into a tight line, and anger began to simmer inside her. She didn't have to have avowals of love from him to know that what they shared was special. She just required the time to prove it to him.

And prove it she would, if it was the last thing she ever did! How dare that man just stand aside and let her walk out of his life? How dare he cut off their relationship before it had a chance to blossom to its full potential? Well, he might be cowardly enough to do so, she decided indignantly, but she was damned if she was going to provide him with the shears!

Her eyes shooting sparks, Shannon tossed her purse and jacket onto a nearby chair and stormed through the open doorway. She had plenty to say to a certain golden-eyed golden-haired moron, and if he didn't like it, he could roar to his heart's content. At least when the words were said she could leave here with her dignity intact, instead of slinking away, licking her wounds like a whipped puppy.

Donovan helped T.J. and Sam load Shannon's luggage into the trunk of his car, and did his best to ignore their reproachful looks. Finally slamming the lid closed with unnecessary force, he glared at them in an excess of temper. "Do you guys have something to say to me?"

Although T.J. pushed forward belligerently, Sam gripped his arm and held him back. "Chill out, man," he whispered to the other boy. "If you tangle with the lion, you know you're going to regret it."

Just then the door to the shelter flew open, and a wild-eyed, redheaded whirlwind stormed down the front stairs and headed in their direction. As Shannon approached the openmouthed trio, T.J. put words to what each of them was thinking. "Geez, she looks fit to murder somebody."

Slipping his hands into the rear pockets of his jeans, Sam rocked back on his sneakered heels and grinned. With a sideways glance at the large, stupefied man beside him, he asked, "Have any idea which of us she's gunning for, Donovan?"

T.J. emitted a sarcastic snicker and dug an elbow into the other boy's ribs. "Who you bettin' on, Sam? I'm placing my dough on Red."

A bit of friendly raillery ensued, but Donovan barely noticed it. He was too busy studying the flushed face of the woman who was approaching him, his amazement heightened by a little kick of excitement. Never once in the two weeks he'd known her had he seen Shannon's usual calm ruffled, not even when she was displeased about something. He had never—ever—seen her lose her cool.

Normally she was in full control of her emotions at all times, calm, serene and unfailingly patient. But apparently her Irish was on the rise, and those milder qualities were being supplanted by ancestral memory. If his eyes weren't deceiving him, she was in the throes of a rip-roaring, hell-bent-for-leather, full-blown temper tantrum. She was magnificent, and just looking at her made his blood run hot.

Donovan crossed his arms over his chest and leaned back against the closed trunk lid. Stretching his legs out in front of him, he fought to suppress a grin as he observed Shannon's stiff-legged gait and the fists that were clenched at her sides. She was a boldly enraged little termagant, he decided with bemused pride. It made him wonder how he could initially have judged her looks to be average. Right now, she had to be the most beautiful woman he had ever seen.

His hungry gaze reinforced that conclusion, wandering over the baggy sweater that effectively concealed her breasts. She was self-conscious about her size in that area, but she had no reason to be. She was round and firm and delicately shaped, fitting into his hands as though she were made for them. And she tasted as sweet as she looked, he remembered, his mouth going dry as a fireburst of sensation flooded his loins with warmth.

The already snug fit of his jeans grew tighter in the crotch, and the muscles in his thighs bunched uneasily. Afraid that his face was doomed to match the color of his red pullover sweater, he quickly shifted his attention away from Shannon's chest. He glanced down, his eyes zeroing in on her colorful leggings, which lovingly clung to every curve they covered. Immediately his own temper rose, and he scowled in disapproval. "Those things are indecent," he snapped.

Shannon plopped her fists onto her hips and gave him a deceptively sweet smile. "If you're referring to my pants, they're in style, and don't try changing the subject!"

Donovan struggled to tear his attention from her shapely limbs, but once he did his expression conveyed his bewilderment. "What subject?"

"Your pigheadedness, for starters."

A distinctly disrespectful guffaw erupted from T.J., and Donovan's threatening gaze pinned him where he stood. Sam quickly began pushing his friend toward the shelter, sparing no more than a conciliatory over-the-shoulder glance at the steely-eyed older man. "We're outa here!"

Donovan's lids narrowed as he shifted his attention to Shannon, who was staring at him with a smirk on her face. Muttering a curse beneath his breath, he grabbed her arm and threw open the door of the car. "So are we," he remarked grimly.

Shannon's protest was halfhearted at best. "I'm not impressed by this macho act, Mr. Lancaster."

"Just get in the damn car, Shannon. If I know those two, they've got their eyes plastered to a window by now, and they see enough violence in the streets without adding us to their list."

Calmly seating herself against the old Ford's worn upholstery, she slanted him a derisive, scorn filled glance. "My, my! In our iron-man mode again, are we?"

Unfortunately for the sake of her composure, as soon as the taunt was uttered, she remembered last using it in regard to Donovan's sexual stamina. And it seemed that his memory was every bit as good as hers, if his resultant howl of laughter was any indication. In the time it took her chuckling, smugly amused nemesis to walk around the car and seat himself beside her, her embarrassment had evolved into a voice-devouring monster.

She swallowed heavily, her heightened color spreading until she felt certain her entire body was on fire. Sneaking a sideways glance at Donovan, she noticed the triumphant curve of his lips with increased frustration. "Don't say a word!" she snapped when he cleared his throat loudly.

Jerking her head around, she kept her eyes glued to the front windshield, as thought the remains of the unidentifiable bug she found splattered there was of the utmost fascination. "Not...one...word!"

But Donovan was unable to resist temptation. With mocking innocence, he asked, "Don't you think we should discuss these peculiar fantasies of yours in greater detail, honey?"

As the engine roared to life and the car began negotiating the road to his cottage, Shannon maintained what she hoped was a dignified silence. She was not sulking, she assured herself staunchly, even as her lower lip pushed forward in a pout. The grinning moron could think what he liked, but she knew the truth. She was in the midst of a glorious rebellion!

And by the time she was through testing her mettle, she vowed, Donovan Lancaster would no longer feel in the least like laughing.

Ten

Shannon paced from one end of Donovan's screen-enclosed back porch to the other, irritably aware of the cold seeping into her bones. They had barely made it inside when the rain had started, and she had headed for the back of the house without consulting him. She hadn't been able to bear the thought of being enclosed by four solid walls, not when she felt ready to jump out of her skin.

She still felt as if her nerves were time bombs ready to explode, and now the possibility of freezing first was adding to her discomfort. Her sweater was bulky, but it was an open-weave knit, that did nothing to lessen the bite of the wind that was howling through the screens. She wished she hadn't discarded her jacket along with her purse before leaving the shelter, but there was no way she was going to ask Donovan for the loan of one of his.

When he had tried to talk her into going back inside the house for their discussion, and she had refused, he had become downright sarcastic. Now she was determined to cut off *his* nose to spite *her* face, or turn into a block of ice trying. Discussions, hah! she thought sourly. Her mind was spinning like crazy, but as yet she hadn't managed to get one word past her chattering teeth.

Where was all her earlier resolution? she wondered in increasing panic. Where was her righteous indignation, her determination to make Donovan see reason? For that matter, where was her poise? So far, all she had accomplished was to make a fool of herself, and that realization did little to ease her tension. It also didn't do much to bolster her flagging self-confidence.

A mocking masculine voice interrupted her thoughts. "Here, you'd better slip one of these on before you turn into a Popsicle."

Shannon jumped and whirled around like a scalded cat. Donovan was standing by the back door, and gesturing toward several garments hanging on a shiny brass coatrack. With increasing indignation, she noticed that he had already taken care of his creature comforts by donning a fleece-lined denim jacket.

Attempting to clench her hands into fists at her sides, she realized they were numb from the cold and stiffly unresponsive. Clumsily crossing her arms over her chest, she surreptitiously tucked her frozen fingers beneath her armpits and glared at him. With a haughty tilt of her head, she refused his offer with a bald-faced lie. "I'm perfectly comfortable, thank you."

"I can see that," he drawled, his tongue clearly planted firmly in his cheek. "The tinge to your mouth is rather an attractive shade of blue, and goose bumps have always turned me on."

"Everything turns you on," she countered sullenly.

Donovan wandered over to a floral-patterned outdoor settee and seated himself with all the aplomb of a man prepared to withstand a lengthy siege. Raising his arms, he linked his fingers together behind his head and leaned back with a grunt of satisfaction. "Mmm...everything in relation to you certainly does."

Shannon glared at him, irritated beyond measure by his casual insouciance. "Do you know what your problem is? You're preoccupied by sex, Donovan Lancaster."

Lowering his arms, he gave his head a decisively negative shake. "It's not sex I'm preoccupied with, honey. It's you."

A disbelieving snort was accompanied by an incredulous arch of her mobile brows. "You're so preoccupied with me, you can hardly wait to slam the door behind me when I leave."

His eyes narrowed, and his inspection of her rebellious features penetrated to the core of her emotions. "Don't talk like an idiot."

So she was an idiot for telling him what she really thought, was she? She'd show him an idiot, and stuff the truth down his throat until he was forced to swallow it or choke to death. "You don't want me complicating your life, remember, Donovan? When it comes right down to it, all you needed was a little sex to satisfy a temporary itch. You were celibate for too long, that was your problem. I suspect that once you've replaced me with another lover, you'll forget me without any difficulty."

He absorbed her confusion and her pain, and the accusation in her voice slammed into him with vicious force. Straightening abruptly, he began an irritated drumming of his fingertips against the wide wooden arm of the settee. "You don't really believe that!"

"Don't I?" Her voice held a bitter inflection. "You certainly haven't done anything to convince me that you ever wanted more than a few hours in bed and a quick goodbye."

His twitching fingers were stilled when he gripped the arm of the settee, his other hand rising to rake through his hair in frustration. "We've had more than good sex together, and you know it as well as I do. But that's not the issue here."

"Then what is?"

Donovan had used every argument he could think of, including a few well-intentioned lies, to convince Shannon they didn't belong together. As a result, she had only ended up thinking that their relationship meant nothing to him. He couldn't go on letting her believe that, any more than he could stomach further deceptions. He had tried to explain, that night on the beach, and he winced inwardly when he remembered how indignant she had become. Well, if he made her angry again, so be it. The time had come for the truth, whether her pride was injured by it or not.

His eyes steely with determination, he said, "Your home in Los Angeles and your nursing career are part of what you are, Shannon. What am I supposed to do, ask you to throw away everything you've worked for to stay here with me?"

His chest heaved on an indrawn breath, which he noisily expelled through clenched teeth. "We have need of a clinic right here at the shelter, and I know if I asked you would stay and run it. For the kids, if not for me."

Shannon stared at him in bemusement, her heart pounding in sudden excitement. "Oh, Donovan. I would."

"No, hear me out," he demanded harshly, one hand raised in a silencing gesture. "This place has a way of inflicting wounds on even the most hardened heart. I don't want yours to break over every child you fail to help, can't you understand that? It would kill me to watch you grow bitter and disillusioned, and to know my selfishness was at the root of your misery.

"Go back home, honey," he urged gently. "Go back to a sane world that will make you happy, not one that will demand too much of you. Dragging our relationship out will only cause more pain, and eventually you'll end up hating me. I would rather lose you now, while you can still smile at me, than later, when all your laughter has been silenced by anguish.''

Shannon's eyes widened in sudden realization, and she burst out with a curse that would have made a dockside sailor proud. "So that's what all of this has been about?" she raged. Although her pacing feet kept time with her volatile tongue, her eyes remained fixed on his stubbornly set features. "You've let that damned protective instinct of yours gain the upper hand, and now you're convinced that you're doing me a favor?

"Well, before you pat yourself on the back, let me tell you about heartbreak, Donovan." Drawing a fortifying breath into her anger-depleted lungs, she slashed the air in front of her with a clenched fist. "A heart breaks when babies are born too soon, and are too weak and underdeveloped to survive for very long. A heart breaks when a little one comes into this world from the body of a drug- or alcohol-dependent mother, and you have to watch helplessly while they writhe in agony and cry for help you can't give them. As one of a critical care team that fights to save those babies, there's nothing I don't know about grief and despair, hopelessness and loss."

His face ashen, he rasped, "I had no idea you did that kind of work, Shannon. I thought—''

She stared at him in stupefaction, suddenly remembering that she had never discussed her specialized training with him. All he had been told was that she was a pediatric nurse. Some of her anger dissipated. But pain over his lack of faith in her gained ascendancy when she realized that he viewed her as some weak, ineffectual namby-pamby, not the resilient, resourceful woman she was.

Pointing an accusing finger in his direction, she said mockingly, "You pictured me ministering to plump, healthy infants and toddlers with shining eyes and adorable smiles?"

He winced at the harshness of her tone, and shrugged uneasily. "That's about the size of it.''

"Nothing could be further from the truth, but in a way you were right about me, Donovan." Her shoulders slumping in defeat, she pressed her fingers against her temples and closed her eyes. "For years I've put my personal life on hold while I concentrated almost solely on my career, but I've only been hiding from the truth about myself."

"And that is?" he questioned curtly.

"That I'm not invincible," she whispered hollowly. "That I can't detach myself from my emotions without paying the price in dignity and self-respect. That I need more from life than a prestigious career and material gain."

"Shannon?"

He waited for her lashes to rise and her gaze to become focused on his face before asking, "What is it you need, honey?"

Moistening her lips with the tip of her tongue, she momentarily braced herself before admitting, "To be more than a woman with a skilled pair of hands and a lonely heart."

Donovan's breath caught at the poignant simplicity of her response, but her statement only increased his concern for her welfare. "And do you really think you can achieve a proper balance here, where every day there's a new battle to face in a never-ending war?"

Shannon nodded in affirmation. "Trina and Sam and the others like them need me, and I need them just as much, Donovan." Pausing for a moment, she stiffened abruptly and said, "Now I'd like to ask you a question, and I would appreciate as honest an answer as possible."

Eyeing her warily, he inclined his head and waited for her to continue. Tense seconds passed while she gathered her courage, but she finally managed to voice the question that was uppermost in her mind. "Do you want me to stay, Donovan?"

Much to her amazement, he didn't attempt to sidestep the issue. Instead, he irritably muttered, "Of course I want you to stay." Leaning forward until his elbows were braced on his knees, he clasped his fingers together and stared down at his hands with unseeing eyes. "No matter how hard I try, I no longer seem to be able to imagine this place without you."

His disgruntled tone made her smile. "Then why try? In case it's escaped your notice, I've already acclimatized myself to life at the shelter. I've seen the kinds of problems you and your staff have to deal with, but I've also seen the good you're accomplishing on a day-to-day basis.

"Even if I lose some of the kids back to the streets," she said earnestly, "they won't ever forget this place, or the people who tried to help them. They will have gained a new perspective about themselves, and hopefully the seeds that were planted here will someday bear fruit. As long as there's life, there's hope for a new beginning, Donovan. I know because that's what I'm looking for—a new beginning."

His head rose, but her heart sank when she saw his obdurate expression. He had made up his mind that she didn't belong at the shelter, and even if she talked herself hoarse, he wasn't going to change it. She could see the doubts shadowing his eyes and the determination firming his lips. Before he opened his mouth, she had already guessed what he was going to say. "I'm still not convinced you could ever find your new beginning here, Shannon."

Something inside her was shattered by his honesty, and she looked at him with dull, lackluster eyes. "And you're not willing to let me try, are you?"

When he remained silent, she stiffened as if she had received a blow, but she kept her head high. "Then I guess there's nothing more to discuss," she said quietly. "If you don't mind, I think it's time for us to pick up my rental car, Donovan. The sooner I go, the better it will be for both of us."

Her words sliced through him like hot knives, and the thought of ending things between them pierced him to the

arrow of his bones. With a muffled curse, he lunged for-
ard and grabbed at her waist. Pulling her onto his lap, he
uried his face between her soft breasts and uttered the plea
e had held back for so long. "Don't leave me, Shannon."

Her arms reached around him to cradle his head, and
hen he experienced their gentleness, he tightened his hold.
Just the thought of losing you has me bleeding to death
side," he muttered self-consciously.

She began to caress his hair in a soothing motion, but the
ating sincerity of his words caused her fingers to falter and
ow still. "What are you saying?" she asked hesitantly.

His head rose, and as they stared at each other, his broad
eekbones turned ruddy with embarrassment. Those won-
rful eyes of his were filled with emotion, and her heart
gan to pound frantically against the wall of her chest.
You need me!" she gasped in sudden realization. "You
ed me, Donovan!"

He scowled at her. "Yes, dammit!"

A joyous burst of laughter erupted from her throat.
Stubborn man," she scolded softly, her breath catching on
sob. "I never thought you'd admit to such a weakness, but
m glad you did."

"That's what a woman like you does to a man," he mur-
ured dryly. "Makes him weak in the head."

"Will it make you feel better to know it's a shared weak-
ss, Mr. Macho?"

Her teasing brought his head up, and his eyes glinted
ickedly. "Oh, yes, but that kind of provocation makes
ore than my head feel weak."

"Oh, too bad. I was kind of hoping..."

The demure fluttering of her lashes didn't fool him a bit.
What do you think I am, some kind of Iron Man?"

"Aren't you?"

Her pouting lips and sultry gaze were all he needed to take
efensive action, and he did so as satisfactorily as she had
oped he would. His lips captured hers in a kiss that min-

gled the sweetness of reverence with the heat of desire
Shannon clung to him with all the pent-up yearning of he
lonely heart, no longer afraid to chance sharing hersel
completely with the man she loved.

In a single surge, Donovan lifted her and rose to his feet
heading back inside the house with flattering speed. Tight
ening her arms around his neck, she spread kisses over ever
inch of his face she could reach. She was laughing and cry
ing at the same time, her tears a soothing balm that healed
a heart that had been close to breaking.

Shannon was no longer cold, but warm—deliciously
warm. By the time they reached his bedroom, Donova
seemed to be as hot as she was. His features were taut with
suppressed passion, and a fine film of perspiration added
luminous quality to his skin. He kicked the door shut with
his heel, his chest rising and falling rapidly to accommo
date his increased heart rate.

Standing her beside his large bed, he began tearing at he
clothes with frustrated haste. Shannon laughed softly as sh
attempted to assist in the removal of his garments, but h
just brushed aside her hands with an impatient mutter. The
he reached for her, and her own clothing melted away with
a speed that amazed and delighted her. When he pulled he
against a body that was rigid and aching with need, sh
melted into him with a tiny sigh of satisfaction.

Donovan felt as if every nerve ending in his body wer
screaming with impatience. He was as starved for her as i
this were their first time together, and maybe, in a way, i
was. Today he had admitted his need to keep her in his life
he thought, which was a commitment of sorts. Certainl
more of a commitment than he had ever imagined himsel
making to any woman, he realized bemusedly.

To his amazement, the realization didn't hinder his ea
gerness in the least, and he jerked back the covers on the be
with a triumphant smile. It was a smile that turned Shan
non's knees to water, and she didn't offer the least resis

tance when he urged her onto cool brown-and-tan plaid sheets. She was shivering all over, but for very different reasons than on the porch. Now, with his furnacelike heat stroking her naked flesh with fingers of fire, she was as primed as a lit fuse.

Positioning his knees between her parted thighs, he lowered himself into the cradle of her hips with a ragged expulsion of breath. Bracing the weight of his upper body on his elbows, he clasp her head in his hands and held her gaze as he began a gentle rocking motion against her. "I shouldn't be doing this right now," he muttered through clenched teeth.

Shannon clutched at his shoulders.. "Oh, yes, you should."

When she wrapped her legs around his hips and twisted against him, he gasped and held very still. Much more of this and he was going to explode, and they still had some details to settle before he lost himself in the welcoming depths of her body. With characteristic stubbornness, he said, "We should be making plans."

But Shannon wasn't in the mood for a lengthy discussion just then. With a murmur of frustration, she tightened her legs around him and closed her eyes, wriggling to achieve the full penetration she desired. "Can't we make love now and discuss details later?"

Donovan barely managed to delay giving her what she wanted...what they both wanted.... His forehead beading with sweat, he fought for control of his breath and his sexual urges. Finally able to draw a decent lungful of air, he gasped, "Look at me, Shannon."

Her lashes lifted with sluggish reluctance, but her gaze sharpened when she noticed the tense lines scoring grooves in his face. As though she were absorbing his unease, she felt her own body stiffen reflexively, and she gazed up at him with worried eyes. "What's wrong?" she whispered.

"I want you to call the hospital immediately and let them know you won't be returning."

Her breath got stuck somewhere between her throat and her lungs, and she could have sworn her heart stopped beating for a moment. "You want to what?"

"You heard me," he said huskily, brushing a caressing thumb against her parted lips. "Now that I've decided to keep you, there doesn't seem much point in waiting to inform your employers."

"Very logically put," she murmured teasingly. "Is practicality your only motivation, Donovan?"

"You know it's not," he whispered wryly. "Will you need a few weeks to work out your notice?"

Her fingers slowly brushed through the hair at the back of his head, and she smiled when he shivered in response. "Not really, since the hospital isn't expecting me back for another three months," she replied with unaccustomed docility. "That will give them plenty of time to replace me, but I will need a few days to clear out my condo, get it listed for sale, and put my furniture in storage."

"Are you certain you want to do this?" he asked, his broad forehead creased with worry lines. "You'll be leaving your family and friends, and everything that's familiar to you. Hell, we haven't even discussed your salary, not to mention health benefits and other pertinent details."

"None of that matters," she said simply. "To stay at the shelter with you, I'd pack up and move to Outer Mongolia."

Donovan stared at her, his throat working convulsively as he tried to swallow. No one had ever made sacrifices for him before, and he couldn't find words to express what he was feeling in that instant. This woman with the gentle eyes and the tender heart had more courage in her little finger, he realized, than he had in his whole body.

She was willing to turn her back on security and everything she had worked for, and she was willing to do so without asking for any promises of a personal nature from him in return. The knowledge both humbled and shamed him, and he buried his face against the soft curve of her neck. "You realize our plans for a clinic might not work out? We'll have to apply to the proper authorities for permission, and there's no guarantee we'll get it."

He didn't see the peacefulness in her expression, or the love light burning in her eyes. Tenderly she cradled his head in her hands and brushed a kiss against his temple. "Then you'll just have to find other work for me to do, and at least you'll have a trained nurse on the premises in case of emergency."

He lifted his head and gazed down at her, concern darkening his eyes. "I hope you don't ever have cause to regret..."

"I won't," she stated, without the slightest hesitation. "There will be no regrets, Donovan."

With a muffled cry, he pressed a burning kiss to her fragrant flesh, and clung to her as if she were his last hope of salvation. His mouth slid to her breast in hungry urgency, while his hips once again began to rock in cadence with hers. His hand slipped between their bodies, and he murmured his approval when he found her soft and wet and ready for him. In a single thrust, he became a part of her, and the world as he had always known it shifted on its axis.

No matter how much Donovan asked of her, Shannon gave to him with unstinting generosity. No matter how much she demanded of him, he satisfied her needs with an enthusiasm that threatened to tear his body apart. They made love with a gentle ferocity that spiraled out of control, each of them seeking more and still more from the other. Higher and higher they climbed, until they reached the peak and fell over the edge into a languid void that existed only for them.

Donovan clung to her in that instant, secure in the sweet haven of her embrace. The world could have fallen apart around him, and he would have neither known nor cared.

Making love with Shannon created a peaceful balm for his restless spirit, and he experienced a sense of rightness in the moment and in the woman he held in his arms. As those arms tightened possessively around her, Donovan didn't realize that he had just taken the first, tentative step toward placing his heart in someone else's keeping.

Shannon stumbled into her living room, a stunned expression on her face, and slowly collapsed into the corner of her lumpy sofa. She curled her legs beneath her, and weakly rested her head against the overstuffed back of the sofa. Frantically calculating certain dates in her mind, she realized that she had been too busy the past couple of months to notice the cessation of a very significant biological function.

But good old Mother Nature was in the process of reminding her, and with a vengeance. This was the third morning in a row that she had lost her breakfast, her breasts were abnormally tender, and lately she'd been almost too tired to place one foot in front of the other. All the signs were there, she decided incredulously, but there had to be some other explanation for her symptoms. There had to be!

She couldn't be pregnant. Six years ago, three separate specialists had been in agreement regarding her condition, and she had no difficulty remembering the mental and emotional pain she had suffered as a result of their prognosis. "Malformed tubes... Widespread tissue blockage... Conception unlikely to occur spontaneously." Those words had been burned into her brain, a continuous reminder that had influenced every decision she had later made for the future. Could the doctors have been wrong?

Shivering convulsively, she wrapped her heavy flannel robe more tightly around her chilled body and closed her eyes. *Don't do this to yourself,* she warned herself silently. *You stopped praying for a miracle a long time ago.*

But even as her mind urged caution, a tiny tendril of hope began to blossom in her heart. "Please, God," she whispered fervently, "please let it be true."

Shannon was so caught up in her thoughts, she failed to hear the knock at her door. But the voice that called to her brought her back to an awareness of her surroundings, and she suddenly remembered the shopping trip she and Trina had planned for this morning. Marriage wasn't proving to be the bed of roses the young girl had envisioned, and Shannon was becoming increasingly worried about her. Since Trina's birthday was only a couple of months away, Shannon had decided to jump the gun a little and buy her some clothes. She was hoping a few bright, fashionable maternity outfits would raise the girl's morale.

Depression was natural during a pregnancy, especially considering the youth of the mother-to-be, but Trina had more than her new household responsibilities to worry about. Shortly after they married and moved into the cottage Donovan had provided for them, Sam had abruptly quit school and taken a job working full-time at a service station in town. Trina had been devastated, and had blamed herself for putting too much pressure on her young husband.

"It's my fault," she'd told Shannon later. "It's my fault he's quitting school and giving up his dream of becoming an engineer. Sam's smart—he would have made it if it weren't for me."

Throwing herself into Shannon's arms, she'd sobbed bitterly. "Now all he'll have to look forward to is a bunch of dead-end jobs he hates. Someday he'll blame me for ruining his life, just like my father blamed my mother for getting pregnant with me. Can't you ask Donovan to talk to him, Shannon?"

Shannon had agreed to discuss the situation with Donovan, but, surprisingly, he had supported Sam's decision. 'He has to do what he feels is best for his family, honey. It wouldn't be right for me to interfere between a man and his wife.''

"It's just so damn frustrating," she'd exclaimed. "Isn't there anything you can do to keep him in school?"

"Right now, no. Sam knows he's going to need every penny he can scrape together to pay Trina's hospital bills when she delivers, and yes, I offered to help, and he refused.''

He'd scowled his disapproval of the boy's obstinacy, and shrugged impotently. "In fact, he's even insisting on paying me rent for his cottage. Although I hated like hell to do it, I finally agreed to let him continue working part-time here to cover the added expense.''

Viewing Shannon's dejected expression, he'd grinned suddenly and caught her in his arms. "Don't worry, I promise I'll help the kids in any way I can. What we have to keep in mind is that Sam is just now realizing the full extent of the burden he's shouldered, and he's running scared. We've got to give him a little time to work through his problems in his own way, Shannon."

He had kept his promise, and Sam was beginning to realize that accepting Donovan's counsel would in no way diminish his authority as head of his own household. He was also realizing that, as his wife, Trina should have a say in any future decisions he might make. The result was more open communication between the young couple, and a deeper level of trust in each other.

Unfortunately, no amount of counseling had been able to diminish the guilt Trina still felt, or her fears for the future. Shannon realized how tough the next couple of years were going to be for Trina and Sam, and she could only pray that their marriage would stand up to the strain. Their love for each other was a very powerful motivating force, but she had more reason than most to know that there were some problems love couldn't solve.

When another series of knocks reverberated against the door, Shannon put aside her musings and got to her feet. "Just a minute, honey."

Crossing the floor on unsteady legs, she released the bolt lock and stood back for Trina to enter. "I'm sorry," the girl gasped as she hurried into the room. "I forgot to set my alarm, and I—"

Trina's explanation was abruptly halted when she turned and took a good look at Shannon. "What's wrong?" she questioned anxiously.

Shannon shrugged dismissively, but a surge of faintness caused her to return to the sofa in double-quick time. Once she was seated, she attempted a reassuring smile in her young friend's direction. "Nothing's wrong. I'm just a little tired, that's all."

Trina bit her lip. Her expression was indecisive as she placed a hand on Shannon's shoulder and sat down beside her. With the blunt honesty of youth, she said, "You look awful!"

Recalling the pasty skin and the shocked eyes that had stared back at her from her bathroom mirror, Shannon silently concurred with Trina's opinion. Uttering a rueful laugh, she gave the hand resting against her shoulder a reassuring pat. "You see what getting old does to a woman?"

Unfortunately, her attempted levity was lost on Trina, who quickly averted her gaze from Shannon's features. Returning her hand to her lap, she began tracing a trembling forefinger across the checks patterning her skirt. She appeared deep in thought, a contemplative frown on her face as she continued worrying her bottom lip with her teeth. Her other hand was pressed against her firmly rounded tummy. As she muttered her next question, her voice wobbled slightly. "Shannon, could . . . could you be pregnant?"

Trina kept her eyes fixed resolutely on her moving finger, and when Shannon noted the embarrassed color that surged into the youngster's cheeks, she was flooded with shame. So much for the care she and Donovan had taken not to flaunt their relationship, she thought in self-disgust. Here she was, a mature thirty-three-year-old woman with at least a modicum of common sense. Yet if what she suspected was true, she was also a woman who had been caught in the oldest trap known to woman.

At least Trina had had the impetuousness of youth to account for her condition. Shannon had no such excuse. After all, her doctors hadn't said that conception was impossible, just that it was very unlikely to occur. As a nurse, she should at least have considered the possibility that nature might triumph over medical science, as she had seen happen often enough in the past. She should have acted more responsibly.

Now she was in the position of holding herself accountable for her actions, and it wasn't easy to admit that as a role model she had failed miserably. Yet to attempt an evasion at this point would be useless, since Trina had asked not if she was pregnant, but if she could be. The girl's trust was important to her, and Shannon's pulse began to run away with her as she struggled to collect her thoughts. Finally she drew in a sharp breath, and decided on total honesty. "I was just sitting here wondering the same thing."

"Then you haven't seen a doctor?"

Shannon leaned her head against the back of the sofa once again and closed her eyes. She felt the cushions give as Trina rose to her feet, but she was too drained to pay much attention. Her eyelids had grown heavy, and her entire body was too lethargic to allow for movement. But when she heard Trina lift the receiver on the phone, her lashes fluttered upward in alarm. "You're not calling Donovan, are you?"

Trina appeared startled, and then distinctly disapproving. "You do intend to tell him, don't you?"

Just the thought was enough to cause her stomach to recoil sickeningly, and she swallowed repeatedly until the nausea eased. How was she ever going to make Donovan understand that she was just as surprised by her impending motherhood as he was certain to be? she wondered uneasily. He was a reasonable man, but, she remembered, he had been manipulated by women in the past. Shannon didn't relish the task ahead of her.

By now thoroughly out of sorts, she muttered, "Of course I intend to tell him!"

Wincing at the petulance in her voice, she added more calmly, "At least I will once I'm certain my symptoms aren't a figment of my imagination." Briefly sketching her medical history for Trina, she whispered, "I want Donovan's baby so much, but sometimes a woman's mind can play tricks on her body. I could be experiencing a false pregnancy, and I can't allow myself to believe otherwise until I visit a doctor."

Smiling in satisfaction, Trina said, "That's why I'm calling mine. As well as working at Fairmont, she has an office on Estudillo in San Leandro for private patients. From what I've been told, and judging by my own experience, she's a top-notch gynecologist. I think you'll like her, Shannon."

Shannon sighed listlessly. As physically enervated as she felt at the moment, she doubted she was capable of taking a liking to anyone.

Shannon placed the last of the supplies in the medicine cabinet Donovan had provided for the clinic, closed and locked the glass-fronted door and stood back to survey her handiwork. A muffled thud sounded behind her, rapidly accompanied by a curse, and she turned to glance at the disgruntled man behind her. With measured footsteps, she sauntered across the recently carpeted cement floor of the cavernous basement area. Her sneakered feet made little or no sound as she stealthily approached his broad back, and looked down at him.

In unnecessarily loud tones, she asked, "Haven't you figured out how to put the cot together yet?"

Donovan's body jerked in surprise, and his head spun around with a rapidity that threatened to crack the bones in his neck. His expression held a distinct element of threat as he muttered, "Don't get cute with me, woman. I'm not in the mood."

Propping her hands on her jean-clad hips, she gave him her most irrepressible grin. "You're always in the mood."

His eyes kindled as he rose to his feet, his tall body shown to advantage in a pair of snug brown cords and a moss green sweatshirt. As he advanced, Shannon retreated, her hands outstretched to fend him off. "Now, Donovan," she exclaimed with a giggle, "we don't have time to play around. The kids will be back from the hardware store in a minute, and you promised to have the infirmary cots assembled and ready by the time they got here."

She nearly managed to escape from the determined male stalking her, but her progress was impeded by a pile of boxes stacked just inside the room. She bumped into them with a startled yelp, lost her balance, and both she and the boxes went tumbling to the floor in a flurry of arms and legs and spilled bedding. Incongruously, her head landed on a soft, foam-filled pillow, and a peal of laughter burst from her as she imagined the comical sight she must present to the man towering over her.

"Are you comfy?" he inquired, his lips twitching betrayingly.

Determined to regain a measure of dignity, Shannon stretched her arms languorously over her head as though she had planned her descent to the floor. The deep breath she drew thrust her breasts upward against her soft beige wool sweater, and she wriggled her hips just a little to get her point across. "Mmm..." she mewled contentedly. "I feel wonderful."

As a pair of golden eyes ignited with sparks, she saw that she had succeeded in upsetting Donovan's equilibrium beyond her wildest expectations. He thoroughly surveyed her feminine attributes before saying hoarsely, "You can say that again!"

The peachy flush on her cheeks and the full, voluptuous pout of her lips drew his gaze, and he groaned aloud at the picture of abandoned, sultry sensuality she presented. Dropping to his knees, he trapped her wrists in his hands and leaned forward to capture her luscious, tempting mouth with his own. His prodding tongue encouraged entry, and she gave him what he wanted with a satisfied moan.

"Told you we shouldn't leave these two alone in here," a young voice muttered.

"For shame, for shame," an older voice joined in. "*Dios mio,* Donovan! If left to you, this clinic would never be ready."

Donovan glared up at Manuel, disconcerted by the unexpected audience blocking the doorway. T.J. and Sam wore open grins, and Trina was obviously struggling to suppress laughter. Manuel, of course, wore the smug expression of a disapproving saint.

"It's just disgraceful, the way these guys have been carrying on," Trina said, with only a slight tremor in her voice.

Sam nodded his head with mock solemnity. "Yeah, a guy can't walk two feet without finding them in a clinch."

"Get it on!" T.J. crowed, and Manuel's gold tooth flashed as he shared a look with the heckler. "First they must visit the priest," he insisted piously, but with a rather devilish undercurrent in his voice.

Donovan's glance swept the unwelcome foursome, his scowl deepening to include all of them. Quickly he jumped to his feet and held out a hand to help Shannon up. "She fell," he told them, and a mottled flush colored his cheekbones when Manuel, Sam and T.J. glanced at him with overt skepticism.

Trina, on the other hand, suddenly rushed forward, every trace of amusement wiped from her face. Cradling her burgeoning belly with instinctive protectiveness, she studied Shannon with fear in her lovely dark eyes. "Are you all right?" she gasped. "You didn't hurt the ba—yourself, did you?"

Shannon paled at the unintentional slip the girl had nearly made, and shot a quick look in Donovan's direction. Fortunately his back was turned, as he was starting across the floor to join Manuel and the boys. Her breath escaped from her parted lips in an unsteady burst of relief. Then she caught sight of Trina's dismayed expression, and she felt as guilty as hell for placing her in the position of having to deceive a man she both loved and respected.

With a smile of apology and reassurance, she bent and dusted off the legs of her jeans. "I'm fine, Trina."

But that wasn't entirely true, she thought sardonically, since she'd spent the past three days trying to figure the best way to tell Donovan about the baby. As it was, a few minutes ago the choice had very nearly been taken out of her hands. How horrible it would have been for him to find out in that manner, with a room full of witnesses to mark the occasion.

The sooner she confessed her secret, the better it would be for everyone concerned. As she started to help Trina clean up the mess on the floor, plans began skittering around in her head like hyperactive mice on a treadmill. She would prepare a delicious meal tonight, with candlelight and wine to mark the occasion. She paused in the act of stuffing a pillow into a box and absentmindedly clutched it to her chest as she gazed dreamily off into space.

Her thoughts fragmented into confusion when she felt a tug on the pillow she was holding, and a deeply amused voice murmured a question in her ear. "Has that thing taken root against your bosom, or have you become particularly fond of it, honey?"

With a gasp, Shannon dropped the article in question, and hectic color suffused her cheeks when Donovan bent down to pick it up. After he placed it in the box with the others, she slanted him a strained smile. "I don't know what in the world is the matter with me," she prattled nervously. "Half the time I'm somewhere out in left field, and the rest I spend wondering what I'm supposed to be doing."

T.J. had begun transferring the supply boxes to the far wall, where they would be stacked and out of the way until the storage chests Donovan was building were completed. Overhearing Shannon's complaint, he lifted his head and smirked at her. "Sounds just like a broad."

Relieved at the distraction the boy's teasing provided, she wrinkled her nose at him. "Sexist!"

"You hear that, Donovan?" he crowed, his teeth a brilliant flash against the darkness of his face. "Shannon thinks I'm sexy."

"Remind me to discuss the difference between *sexist* and *sexy* with you, T.J." he remarked with a pointed glance. "It's a lesson every man has to learn if he hopes to coexist with the female of the species, son."

The affectionate term sent Shannon's mind spinning into the stratosphere again. While Donovan left her to assist T.J. with his task, she watched him cross the room and wondered if she would give him a son. A quiver of delight coursed through her at the possibility, as she envisioned a tiny boy with gold hair and eyes and his daddy's smile. When she finally joined the others, there was a luminescent glow on her face that only Trina recognized and understood.

Eleven

___

Donovan felt anticipation building as he unlocked the front door and stepped inside the cottage. Delicious odors drifted to him from the direction of the kitchen, and he speculated about what Shannon had in store for him tonight. She had left the shelter early to prepare dinner, with an air of suppressed excitement about her that pricked at his curiosity. As he hung his jacket in the coat closet, he wondered what she was up to now.

A grin twitched the corners of his mouth as he realized that this wasn't the first time he'd had such thoughts in the two months he and Shannon had been together. She was delightfully spontaneous, irritatingly unpredictable, and quite often fascinatingly perverse. What she wasn't was boring, and he had long since decided that his life was far richer because he had her in it. To his way of thinking, he was happier and more contented than he had any right to be.

His only dissatisfaction with their relationship arose from her refusal to move in with him. She was adamant about their maintaining separate residences—arguing that they should provide a good example for the kids at the shelter. It was an inconvenience that was beginning to annoy him far more than he thought it would. They spent every evening together, and he saw her for brief periods during the day, but he was increasingly surprised at himself for failing to be satisfied with bits and pieces of her time.

He wanted it all! When she was cuddled in his arms, her body soft and yielding beneath a warm cocoon of blankets, he wanted to be able to hold her through the night. He resented like hell having to get up, get dressed and brave the capricious winter temperatures to return her to the shelter. When he reached out for her in his sleep, he didn't want to wake up to find himself clutching a pillow. It was her face he wanted to see first thing in the morning and last thing at night.

Even more important, to his way of thinking, was his impermanence in her life. He had no real say in where she went, what she did, or who she did it with. Only a more formal relationship, such as that of a fiancé or a husband, provided a man with the opportunity to question a woman's movements with impunity. The thought startled him so much that he began to feel claustrophobic. Since he was still standing inside his guest closet, he supposed his gut reaction was understandable.

Backing quickly out of the confining area, he shut the door and ran suddenly moist palms down the legs of his dusty cords. Clamping down on the randomness of his thoughts, he tried to zero in on the most prevalent cause of his disquiet. It wasn't that he didn't admire Shannon's independent spirit, he told himself. Far from it. But on occasion the woman didn't show a satisfactory amount of concern for her own welfare.

Take that incident just last week, for example. If Shannon had been home with him where she belonged, it would never have happened. She had received a phone call around three o'clock in the morning, and without waking anyone else she had taken one of the shelter's vans and disappeared until midmorning. By the time she had returned home, with one of their frequent boarders in tow, he had been frantic, imagining all the horrors which could befall her in some of the less salubrious areas of Oakland.

When the rescued girl had begun bragging about Shannon's nose-to-nose confrontation with a pimp who was a bit too physically aggressive while trying to solicit the services of the teenager for his stable of prostitutes, Donovan had thought his hair would turn white on the spot. He had sputtered and fumed and ranted and raved, and all to no avail.

Shannon had merely given him a reproving look, smiled sweetly and shrugged her shoulders unconcernedly. "Charmaine needed me," she said. "That jerk has been hassling her for months, and it was time to put a stop to it. He makes it a habit to prey on frightened, vulnerable young girls, Donovan. He takes them in under the guise of friendship, and then forces them to do things his way. If they refuse, he has particularly brutal ways of getting even. The last time he threatened Charmaine, I told her to call me if he gave her any more trouble."

A slow, satisfied smile curved her Cupid's bow of a mouth as she added, "Don't worry. He won't be bothering her anymore."

"No, he'll probably set his sights on you now. You little fool, I swear you don't have the sense God gave a flea. You should have let me handle him."

"In a way, I did," she informed him impishly.

His eyelids narrowed in suspicion. "What do you mean?"

"The word on the street is that no one fools with the lion," she said, a distinct note of pride in her voice. "So I told him I was Donovan Lancaster's woman, and he immediately underwent a remarkable attitude adjustment.

"So did Charmaine," she tossed over her shoulder as she turned to leave. "She decided it would be safer to become a permanent resident at the shelter, so I assigned her to Trina's old room. Is that all right with you?"

His mouth opened, but not a single sound emerged. Since he had been trying to make the recalcitrant youngster see sense for the past six months, there wasn't a whole lot he could say. Instead, he watched Shannon saunter off, and merely shook his head at the combination of irritation and reluctant admiration he felt.

Grinning at the memory, Donovan paused in the entry to the dining room and absently noted the pristine white linen cloth draping the table. There were tapered candles in silver holders centered on the linen surface, and between them stood an elegantly arranged floral centerpiece. Resting his arm on the tall, curved back of one of his pine dining chairs, he sighed heavily and wondered what Shannon was up to now. His features contorted into a frown.

He was doing too much of that lately, he realized inconsequentially. If he wasn't careful, he was going to end up with wrinkles on his face deep enough to qualify as gorges. Was it any wonder? he asked himself, feeling a distinct twinge of self-pity. He wasn't used to dealing with a feisty little redhead who forged paths where any self-respecting angel would fear to tread. The woman thought with her heart, not her head—that was the problem. And her heart was big enough to take on any challenge, be it a troubled teen or a jaded, cynical male with numerous Keep Off signs posted around his heart.

Just then a sweetly melodious voice burst into song, and his frown was immediately replaced by a smile. Straightening with eager anticipation, he traversed the short distance to the kitchen and pushed open the swinging door. Standing in the threshold, he watched the blur that was Shannon as she scurried from the stove to the sink and back again. "Is this a private concert, or can you use a mediocre bass?"

With a surprised gasp, she whirled around, and then she hurled herself at him with a squeal of delight. Her peach wool dress clung to every curve of her slender body. The color should have clashed horribly with her hair, but it didn't. Lifting her up until her feet dangled above the floor, Donovan marveled at how deliciously soft and warm and welcoming she felt. Her arms slipped around his neck, and she seemed to melt against the harder contours of his masculine frame as though fashioned expressly for him. He sighed his satisfaction.

Shannon eagerly spread a string of kisses all over his face, her lips lingering at one corner of his smiling mouth. "You're home early."

His smile deepened, and he angled his head just far enough to savour the taste of her kiss. "You promised to do painful things to my poor, defenseless body if I was late, so I thought I'd give myself enough time to shower before dinner. I didn't want to take the chance of having my most manly attribute disturbed."

Tightening her hold on him, she grinned irrepressibly. "I thought you liked me to disturb your manly attribute."

Setting her on her feet, he slid his hands over her pertly rounded bottom and pressed her against the betraying bulge in his pants. "Now that you mention it, I—"

"Oh, no you don't, mister!" Wriggling out of his embrace, she shook an admonishing finger at him. "First you shower, then we eat the fabulous dinner I've prepared, and then—"

"You get to have your way with my poor defenseless body?" he interjected hopefully.

"Then I have some news I want to share with you." Laughing at his woebegone expression, she said persuasively, "We can cuddle on the love seat in the library while we talk. The fire's all laid and ready to be lit."

"So is mine," he muttered, reaching for her with a stubborn glint in his eye.

Backing away hurriedly, she grabbed a wooden spoon om the butcher-block counter in the center of the room nd waved it at him. "Down, boy! I thought lions pre-rred rare meat, but if you would rather have well-done rime rib, it's okay by me."

He halted in midstride, an interested expression in his es. "Prime rib?"

"Mm-hmm, with roasted carrots and potatoes and lots of ch, thick gravy to spoon over..." Since she was already eaking to an empty room, Shannon didn't bother to mplete her sentence.

Time stood still as Donovan stared down at Shannon in isbelief. She lay against him, with her head resting in the ook of his shoulder. The single lamp in the corner was rned to its lowest setting, and most of the illumination in e cozy library came from the flames leaping in the fire-lace. The dusky light was adequate enough for Shannon to ew the face so near to her own, which at that moment held curiously closed expression. "What did you say?" he uestioned in a careful monotone.

"I . . . we're going to have a baby," she whispered.

A burst of joy unlike anything he had ever experienced cketed through Donovan with mind-numbing force, and e arms that held Shannon tightened reflexively. A child, e thought incredulously, every muscle in his body tensing t the enormity of what he had just learned. His ild . . . created from the love he and Shannon felt for each ther. A blessed miracle, which would bring him and Shan-on closer together than he had ever thought possible.

A miracle, a sudden, insidious inner voice taunted, *or the sult of a well executed plan?* He suddenly recalled all the mes in his life he had trusted the people he loved, only to e betrayed over and over again. His grandfather had used im as proof of his immortality, his parents as the means to

continue their decadent life-style, and the women he'•
known as the goose that laid the golden eggs.

Had Shannon been lying about her inability to conceive
in order to trap him into marriage? The suspicion sickene(
him, and ate at the fragile fabric of the trust he had begu
to have in her. Was this yet another betrayal he would hav•
to endure, or did the love she professed to feel for him re
ally exist? He couldn't be sure, and the knowledge of hi
vulnerability angered him as nothing else could have.

With precisely measured movements, he slipped his arm
from around her shoulders and rose to his feet. He got as fa
as the stone fireplace, then leaned forward and braced both
hands against the framed oak mantel. Shannon felt hi
withdrawal both physically and mentally, and the nebulou
fear she had experienced at the thought of telling him abou
the baby exploded into abject terror.

In the space of a heartbeat, he had once more become th•
cold, unyielding stranger she had hoped never again to see
She had been prepared for him to be shocked at her news
but she hadn't anticipated the anger she could feel emanat
ing from him. The muscles in his back were rigid as h•
gripped the wooden surface of the mantel; his head wa
bowed, as though he held the weight of the world on hi
shoulders.

Donovan laughed, and it wasn't a pleasant sound. "S(
that's what tonight was all about."

Her voice constricted from the tension blocking her vo
cal cords, she asked, "Is that all you have to say?"

Ignoring the question, he glanced at her over his shoul
der. "How far along are you?"

Clearing her throat, she attempted to meet his rapie
glance with studied calm. "Nine weeks."

His eyebrows rose in astonishment. "You conceived dui
ing the first week we began sleeping together? For a woma
who was supposedly sterile, that counts as quite a feat."

Color flooded her cheeks, and just as quickly drained away. Her voice edged with desperation, she pleaded. "I was honest with you, Donovan. The doctors weren't at all optimistic, and I really *didn't* think it was possible for me to have a baby."

"I'll just bet you didn't," he muttered with marked decision.

Pushing himself away from the mantel, he turned to face her. Shannon's heart sank as she took note of the suspicion in his eyes, and the bitterness that twisted his mouth into a caricature of a smile. "I swear it's the truth, Donovan."

She pleated her fingers together in her lap. "I can't blame you for being angry with me, but can't you try to see this situation from my viewpoint?"

Oh, he saw, all right! He saw that he had been played for a sucker from the very beginning. Donovan suddenly felt a mingled rage and pain so great he wanted to scream his agony aloud. Shannon's demure, repentant act was almost believable, he decided with growing hostility, but then, she was a superb performer. When he remembered how easily he had been taken in by her eagerness to pull up stakes and rearrange her life to be with him, he felt like throwing up.

The long and short of it was that he had trusted her, and she had betrayed that trust. Admittedly she had been subtler and less direct in furthering her ambitions, but in the end, her patience had paid off. *God!* How many times does a man have to be emotionally castrated before he learns his lesson? he wondered in burgeoning self-disgust.

A woman would go to any lengths to get what she wanted, he thought derisively. His own mother had taught him that before he was out of diapers, and every woman since had exchanged her favors for a taste of his wealth. All except Shannon, who had been cleverer and more calculating than any female he had come across to date. She had been brave enough to take a chance, to risk a ride on Mother Nature's

carousel in hopes of snatching a shiny ring at the end of he
ride.

Unnerved by his silent appraisal, Shannon scooted to
ward the edge of the love seat. She had spent the past few
minutes trying to decipher his expression, but his hardened
features had given away nothing of his thoughts. Moisten
ing her mouth with the tip of her tongue, she whispered hi
name pleadingly. With a sarcastic curl of his lips, he stud
ied her flaming red hair and remarked drily, "You really d
have the luck of the Irish, sweetheart."

The endearment dripped with sarcasm, and her body
jerked reflexively. Jumping to her feet, she cried, "What ar
you implying?"

"I'm saying that you've played your cards brilliantly, an
ended up with a winning hand, Shannon."

Her eyes grew wide, a dawning horror in their depths
"And just what have I won?" she whispered faintly.

"Marriage to me, and all the material gain that goes with
it."

"You think I planned this baby to trap you into marry
ing me?"

His reaction was everything she had feared. Yet she wasn'
prepared for the silent inclination of his head, nor the
sneering emphasis in his voice as he said, "There are too
many holes in your story for me to believe otherwise."

Bile rose in her throat, threatening to choke her. She wa
almost relieved by the sudden surge of anger she felt. When
she spoke, her low tones were harsh with recrimination. "
shouldn't have to defend myself to you, Donovan. It seem
I'm guilty until proven innocent in your eyes, and all I have
to go on is my word. If that isn't enough for you, the
there's nothing more to talk about."

"There's my baby," he snapped defensively. "I'd say
that's a very important topic of discussion, and you can be
damn sure that I intend to be around to raise him."

Tilting her chin defiantly, she gazed at him with steely determination. "I won't marry you."

"If you refuse, then I'll sue you for custody."

Shannon felt violated, as though Donovan had used his fists against her instead of scornful threats. Her lashes drifted down to conceal the pain in her eyes, and when she turned and began walking away, her body felt stiff and uncoordinated. Instinctively she wrapped her arms around her stomach, in an attempt to shield the innocent life in her womb from anguish.

"Where in the hell do you think you're going?" a grating voice called out to her.

Somewhere along the outer edges of her brain she recognized Donovan's commanding tones, and she automatically paused in the doorway. But, much to her relief, her numbed mind was already beginning to shut him out of her consciousness, as she knew she had to shut him out of her life. Quietly, as if too much sound would shatter her tenuous control beyond repair, she murmured, "I'm going home."

"I'll take you back to the shelter later," he muttered impatiently. "Right now we have several matters we need to talk about."

"I've had all the discussion I can stomach for one night, thank you very much."

"You're behaving like a child," he told her accusingly.

Shannon heard the muffled thud of his footsteps against the carpet, and she whirled around to face him before he could get any closer. Cringing against the edge of the open doorway, she gasped, "Don't touch me!"

The panic in her voice halted Donovan in his tracks, and he stared at the white-faced woman in front of him with growing uncertainty. Her expression was wild, her lips quivering uncontrollably, and her eyes . . . her eyes held an expression he had prayed never to see again. It was a look he had often glimpsed in his mirrored reflection, and in the eyes of countless numbers of G.I.'s who had experienced the bloody carnage of guerrilla warfare. It was a look of shattered innocence and hopeless despair. It was a look into hell!

What have I done? he thought, as remorse rose inside him in a relentless tide. *Dear God in heaven, what have I done?*

Twelve

Wind and rain slashed viciously at Shannon as she ran from pain and disillusion and heartbreak. She heard Donovan calling to her from the darkness, and she increased her pace to escape his pursuit. She was breaking one of his cardinal rules by being out on the grounds alone at this time of night, she thought bitterly, and the only reason he was following her was out of a misguided sense of responsibility. He didn't want her. That was the only reality she knew, and the only reality she couldn't bring herself to accept.

Veering from the illuminated path, she sought the cover of the trees that edged the south side of the estate. Her hair clung to her scalp in a sodden mass, falling over her eyes and blinding her. She stumbled and fell, scraping her knees and hands on the bracken-strewn ground. Sobs tore from her chest, hurting her, constricting her breathing. Thunder roared in the distance, and a bolt of lightning ripped apart the dark, sullen sky.

The acrid smell of rotting vegetation stung her nostrils, and she began to gag. Huddling close to the ground, she retched helplessly, her stomach disgorging its contents while the wrath of ancient gods tore at her defenseless body. Stinging needles of rain penetrated her clothing, leaving her feeling as if her flesh were encased in ice. She began to cough, the spasms increasing in intensity as she staggered to her feet and sought a way out of this eerie, terrifying place of shadows.

She didn't know how long she walked. It might have been minutes or hours, her feverish brain carrying her further into a realm of endless confusion. Trees became monstrous denizens of childhood nightmares, their branches claws that gouged and tore at her exposed flesh with demonic intent. The howling wind seemed to be screaming a warming, crying out her name over and over again, in an endless litany of doom.

Her strength nearly exhausted, she didn't fight the claws that reached up from the bowels of the earth to drag her into the netherworld. Agony speared into her ankle and up through her leg, matching the vicious pain of hot knives slicing into her chest. Her hands clutched empty air, seeking warmth and comfort and safety. "Donovan," she whispered as she became one with the blackness. "Donovan," she sighed as she disappeared into the void.

The presence was back again, calling out to her, trying to get her to leave the peaceful haven she had found. Shannon tried not to listen, but her mind persisted in thwarting her efforts. Restlessly she tossed her head from side to side, but she was unable to escape from the words. Words of love and need and desire, words of anguish and remorse and fear. Words that pummeled her defenses, making her tremble with a nameless longing.

"Don't leave me," the presence pleaded.

Shannon tried to lift her hand to ward off the seductive voice, but something gripped her fingers in a warm vise. "Let me go," she cried, struggling to free herself. "Please let me go."

Again the voice called to her, a painful reminder of something she knew she must forget. "Stay with me, my love."

"No..." she whimpered.

But the presence was stronger than she was, and she was pulled back from the edge of the void by a desperate plea. "Stay...stay...stay..." The words echoed relentlessly in her mind, and she was too tired to go on fighting them.

A paroxysm of coughing tore through her, and she struggled for breath. "It hurts!" she gasped. "It hurts!"

"Use the pain," the presence advised. "Let it strengthen you, Shannon."

Pain seeping into her soul, angry words, golden eyes filled with contempt... Tears flooded beneath her lids and bled through lashes that were too heavy to lift. She didn't want to remember, but pictures were forming in her brain irrespective of her wishes. There was a big, ugly-beautiful house, filled with shouts of laughter, discord and peace. There was a headless chicken, featherless wings flapping around in a huge metal cauldron. And there were faces— young faces with old eyes, and an old face with young eyes. And there was the face of the man she loved more than life itself.

A name came to mind, and she murmured it on a moan. "I'm here," the presence reassured her. "I'll always be here for you, sweetheart."

Once again her head shifted from side to side, this time in denial. "No...promises..." she said with difficulty. "No forever..."

"You are my forever, Shannon."

The voice was fading, growing dimmer as exhaustion settled over her with the heaviness of a shroud. Other sounds came to block out the presence, familiar sounds, comforting sounds. A woman's soothing tones, soft-soled shoes swishing across a linoleum floor, the steady beep-beep-beep of a heart monitor, the rattle of a gurney being rolled across a hallway. She was in a hospital, but she didn't hear babies crying. Why weren't they crying?

A woman screamed, "My baby!"

Shannon struggled to open her eyes, but she didn't recognize the stranger bending over her. "Your baby is fine," he murmured gently. "Sleep now...sleep."

She sighed and allowed her tense body to relax. She was floating on a cloud, as light as thistledown, and all around her was the magic of moonglow. A warm breeze caressed her face, and her lips tingled as though from a lover's kiss. She smiled as she drifted into healing slumber, and failed to hear the presence whisper, "I love you, little flame. I'll always love you."

Last night Shannon had once again turned down his marriage proposal, and Donovan was nearly at the end of his rope. Here it was nearly Christmas, and the stubborn woman still refused to believe that he really loved her and wanted her to become his wife. She maintained that there was absolutely no need for him to feel honor-bound to marry her, just because she was pregnant with his child.

His child. A smile tugged at his lips as he glanced down at the oak cradle he had been sanding to a fine finish, his thoughts turned inward. In a little more than six months he was going to be a father, and he was determined to be prepared. He had been haunting bookstores for material on pregnancy, childbirth and early childhood development.

He knew all about morning sickness, hormonal changes in an expectant mother that more often than not caused increased sensitivity and spurts of irritability, and excessive tiredness. He knew about swollen ankles and backaches. He knew about strange food cravings and when to expect fetal movement. What he didn't know was how to get his child's mother to share this time with him.

When Shannon had awakened to full consciousness in the hospital, she hadn't remembered the four agonizing, horrific days and nights when he had kept a vigil at her bedside. But he remembered. Dear God, he remembered only too well how close he had come to losing her. As the seconds and minutes and hours crawled past, he had begun to believe in forever. Forever empty, forever lonely, forever lost, as he would be without her.

He had listened to her rasping, pain-racked breathing as she relapsed into pneumonia, his own chest tight with suppressed grief and fear as he prayed for a second chance. A chance to live with her by his side. A chance to raise their child together. A chance to grow old loving each other.

Donovan had thought he had experienced terror before, but memories of Vietnam had faded into insignificance when he felt Shannon slipping away from him. Except to shower and shave and occasionally eat a meal, he had refused to leave her side. Even when her parents arrived to share his vigil, Donovan couldn't bear to let her out of his sight. The doctor had ordered a cot brought into her room, and together he and Shannon had fought the battle for her life.

On the fifth day, when she had opened her eyes and immediately asked about the baby, he had assured her that their child was safe. Then he had broken down and cried, begging her over and over again to forgive him. Being the warm, generous-hearted woman she was, she had held him in her arms and offered him the absolution his guilty heart craved. That was the last time she had willingly touched him.

From that day on, they must have discussed every inconsequential subject in the book. Shannon had laughed and joked with Debra and Tricia and a steady stream of visitors from the shelter, but when they were alone she had withdrawn behind a barrier he hadn't been able to penetrate. The first time he proposed to her, she had simply studied his features for a long, tension-fraught moment, and then, calmly and unemotionally, turned him down.

The distant, withdrawn look in her eyes had warned him not to press the matter, and he had cravenly directed their conversation into less controversial channels. Yet it wasn't until she was released from the hospital that he had fully realized how drastically their relationship had changed.

His first hint had come when he'd wanted her to convalesce at his place, and she had insisted upon returning to the shelter. He had acceded to her wishes without an argument, establishing a pattern that was slowly driving him out of his mind. With each day that passed, she was drawing further away from him, and he didn't know how much longer he could tolerate the coldness between them.

The door to his workshop opened, and a face appeared in the aperture. "Come on in, Sam," he called out. "I could sure use some company."

Sam closed the door behind him, and wandered over to the workbench. Nodding toward the cradle, he said, "That's coming along good. Trina's been after me to make one for our kid, but I flunked woodshop."

"I can help you build one," Donovan offered with a grin, "but you'd better get a move on. Your baby's not going to wait until it's finished, you know."

When the boy didn't respond, Donovan glanced over at him and paused in his sanding. Sam looked worried and preoccupied, his shoulders hunched, his hands fiddling nervously with a few stray tools spread across the bench. "I get the feeling you didn't come out here for a chat, son," he said. "What's up?"

Sam's head jerked up, and after a moment of indecision he muttered, "It's Shannon."

Donovan slanted him a glance, his expression carefully controlled. "What about her?"

"She's planning to split," the youngster blurted out. "You can't let her go, Donovan." He let loose with a low moan and shook his head. "Man! Trina will come unglued if Shannon takes off now. Can't you make her stay?"

Donovan's hand curled around the sandpaper, crumpling it into a ball. "How do you know she's leaving?"

"I was walking down the hallway a few minutes ago, and her door was open a crack. She has clothes spread out everywhere, and I spotted a couple of suitcases by the couch."

With a muffled curse, Donovan threw the mangled sandpaper against the far wall and spun on his booted heel. He was out of the door and into his car in about thirty seconds flat, his heartbeat slamming against the wall of his chest in an angry rhythm. She was leaving him, he thought incredulously, struggling to subdue the sickness curdling in his stomach. Without warning, without a word of farewell, she was planning to sneak off into the night and disappear from his life.

Over his dead body!

Shannon was bent over the couch, carefully folding a denim skirt, when her door flew open and bounced against the wall. With a startled scream she spun around, her eyes widening when she saw Donovan framed in the doorway. "What do you think you're doing?" she gasped.

Catching hold of the door with the heel of his boot, he slammed it shut and advanced on her. "Stopping you."

He eyed the piles of clothing, and without another word he sidestepped her and swept them off the couch. She grabbed his arm, and as he strode into her bedroom he dragged her along with him. "Have you gone crazy?" she cried.

"You might say that."

His expression complacent, he crossed the room and dumped the load he carried on the closet floor. With a flick of his wrists and a satisfied grunt, he slid the louvered shutters closed and turned to face the openmouthed Shannon. Dusting off his hands, he eyed her expectantly. "There. What do you have to say about that?"

She simply blinked at him. "You've gone bananas."

"With just cause," he muttered grimly.

Hungrily his glance roamed upward, over her bare legs and her robed figure, to the hair curling riotously over her small head. A few tendrils dusted her cheeks, and he noticed that they were slightly damp. His gaze sharpened when he realized she'd recently showered, and he wondered what she had on under that silky piece of witchery she was wearing.

Shannon knew that look only too well, and she began to back slowly away from him. "Now, Donovan . . ."

"You bet your booty it's going to be now, woman. God knows I've waited long enough for you to come to your senses."

"I don't know what you're talking about."

Step by step he stalked her, until further retreat was prevented by the edge of the bed. With a definite leer, he crossed his arms over his chest. His sparkling gaze conveyed his satisfaction with her predicament. "I'm talking about commitment and forever, Shannon. I'm talking about promises, and trust, and a man who is going to love you until the day he dies and beyond. I'm talking about you and me, dammit!"

Her eyes grew round, a slight mistiness enhancing their emerald depths. "You don't really want me," she said quietly. "You just feel guilty."

"Yes," he admitted, with a curt nod and a tightening of his lips. "I've been carrying around a load of guilt, and it's killing me."

"You . . . you already apologized for the things you said to me," she reminded him. "And it was my fault I ended up pregnant, not yours."

"Are you sorry?" he inquired stiffly. "About the baby, I mean?"

"Of course not," she exclaimed indignantly. "I want this baby, Donovan."

"And the baby's father?" He held out his hand, and his eyes beseeched her. "Do you want him, too?"

Shannon stared down at his upraised palm. Hesitantly, as if a sudden movement would cause him to disappear, she rested her fingers within his warm clasp. "I love you," she whispered.

As if those three words were the only ones that mattered—as indeed they were—she looked up at him and repeated, "I love you, Donovan."

He exhaled audibly and took the final step that would put an end to the distance between them. As he drew her into his arms, he asked, "You won't leave me?"

The hint of insecurity in his voice touched her emotions in a way that brought a lump to her throat. This big, confident man with the roar of a lion had the heart of a lamb, she thought tenderly, and the fear of a child who had been left alone too many times. "I never intended to leave you. I just needed time to recover and I needed to be certain that you really wanted me, not that you felt sorry for hurting me."

Pulling away slightly, he stared down at her in confusion. "But you were packing."

"Maria and Drew are stopping by later to pick up the clothes you just threw in the closet," she admitted with a grin. "They're some things I'm donating to FACES."

Bending his head, he began nibbling away at the impudent smile. "How much later?" he asked huskily.

Shannon closed her eyes, a dreamy expression on her face. "Does it matter?"

As he lowered her to the bed, a hint of his old arrogance could be heard in the lion's growl. "Hell, no! It won't hurt them to hang around for a while. I've been waiting for your love all my life, and I am not a patient man."

"I know," she murmured complacently. "I know, my darling."

*   *   *   *   *

TAKE A WALK ON THE
DARK SIDE OF LOVE WITH

October is the shivery season, when chill winds blow and
shadows walk the night. Come along with us into a haunting
world where love and danger go hand in hand, where
passions will thrill you and dangers will chill you. Silhouette'
second annual collection from the dark side of love brings
you three perfectly haunting tales from three of our most
bewitching authors:

Kathleen Korbel
Carla Cassidy
Lori Herter

Haunting a store near you this October.

by Ann Major

Take a walk on the wild side with Ann Major's sizzling
stories featuring Honey, Midnight...and Innocence!

IN SEPTEMBER, YOU EXPERIENCED...

WILD HONEY Man of the Month
A clash of wills set the stage for an electrifying romance for
J. K. Cameron and Honey Wyatt.

NOW ENJOY...

WILD MIDNIGHT November 1993
Heat Up Your Winter
A bittersweet reunion turns into a once-in-a-lifetime adventure for
Lacy Douglas and Johnny Midnight.

AND IN FEBRUARY 1994, LOOK FOR...

WILD INNOCENCE Man of the Month
One man's return sets off a startling chain of events for
Innocence Lescuer and Raven Wyatt.

Let your wilder side take over with this exciting series—only from
Silhouette Desire!

Silhouette Books has done it again!

Opening night in October has never been as exciting! Come watch as the curtain rises and romance flourishes when the stars of tomorrow make their debuts today!

Revel in Jodi O'Donnell's STILL SWEET ON HIM—
Silhouette Romance #969
...as Callie Farrell's renovation of the family homestead leads her straight into the arms of teenage crush Drew Barnett!

Tingle with Carol Devine's BEAUTY AND THE BEASTMASTER—
Silhouette Desire #816
...as legal eagle Amanda Tarkington is carried off by wrestler Bram Masterson!

Thrill to Elyn Day's A BED OF ROSES—
Silhouette Special Edition #846
...as Dana Whitaker's body and soul are healed by sexy physical therapist Michael Gordon!

Believe when Kylie Brant's McLAIN'S LAW—
Silhouette Intimate Moments #528
...takes you into detective Connor McLain's life as he falls for psychic—and suspect—Michele Easton!

Catch the classics of tomorrow—*premiering* today—
only from ▼ *Silhouette*

KEEGAN'S HUNT
by Dixie Browning

In November, Silhouette Desire has something very special for you—KEEGAN'S HUNT by Dixie Browning, Book One of her wonderful new series, *Outer Banks.*

In KEEGAN'S HUNT, infuriating yet irresistibly sexy ex-military man Richmond Keegan lands on Coronoke Island and immediately drives single mother Maudie Winters crazy...with desire!

Don't miss KEEGAN'S HUNT (#820) by Dixie Browning— only from Sihouette Desire.

**And now for
something completely different
from Silhouette....**

Every once in a while, Silhouette brings you a
book that is truly unique and innovative, taking
you into the world of paranormal happenings.
And now these stories will carry our special
"Spellbound" flash, letting you know that you're
in for a truly exciting reading experience!

In October, look for *McLain's Law* (IM #528)
by Kylie Brant

Lieutenant Detective Connor McLain believes
only in what he can see—until Michele Easton's
haunting visions help him solve a case...and her
love opens his heart!

McLain's Law is also the Intimate Moments
"Premiere" title, introducing you to a debut
author, sure to be the star of tomorrow!

Available in October...only from
Silhouette Intimate Moments

SILHOUETTE.... Where Passion Lives

Don't miss these Silhouette favorites by some of our most popular authors!
And now, you can receive a discount by ordering two or more titles!

Silhouette Desire®

#05751	THE MAN WITH THE MIDNIGHT EYES	BJ James	$2.89 ☐
#05763	THE COWBOY	Cait London	$2.89 ☐
#05774	TENNESSEE WALTZ	Jackie Merritt	$2.89 ☐
#05779	THE RANCHER AND THE RUNAWAY BRIDE	Joan Johnston	$2.89 ☐

Silhouette Intimate Moments®

#07417	WOLF AND THE ANGEL	Kathleen Creighton	$3.29 ☐
#07480	DIAMOND WILLOW	Kathleen Eagle	$3.39 ☐
#07486	MEMORIES OF LAURA	Marilyn Pappano	$3.39 ☐
#07493	QUINN EISLEY'S WAR	Patricia Gardner Evans	$3.39 ☐

Silhouette Shadows®

#27003	STRANGER IN THE MIST	Lee Karr	$3.50 ☐
#27007	FLASHBACK	Terri Herrington	$3.50 ☐
#27009	BREAK THE NIGHT	Anne Stuart	$3.50 ☐
#27012	DARK ENCHANTMENT	Jane Toombs	$3.50 ☐

Silhouette Special Edition®

#09754	THERE AND NOW	Linda Lael Miller	$3.39 ☐
#09770	FATHER: UNKNOWN	Andrea Edwards	$3.39 ☐
#09791	THE CAT THAT LIVED ON PARK AVENUE	Tracy Sinclair	$3.39 ☐
#09811	HE'S THE RICH BOY	Lisa Jackson	$3.39 ☐

Silhouette Romance®

#08893	LETTERS FROM HOME	Toni Collins	$2.69 ☐
#08915	NEW YEAR'S BABY	Stella Bagwell	$2.69 ☐
#08927	THE PURSUIT OF HAPPINESS	Anne Peters	$2.69 ☐
#08952	INSTANT FATHER	Lucy Gordon	$2.75 ☐

	AMOUNT	$ _____
DEDUCT:	10% DISCOUNT FOR 2+ BOOKS	$ _____
	POSTAGE & HANDLING	$ _____
	($1.00 for one book, 50¢ for each additional)	
	APPLICABLE TAXES*	$ _____
	TOTAL PAYABLE	$ _____
	(check or money order—please do not send cash)	

To order, complete this form and send it, along with a check or money order for the total above, payable to Silhouette Books, to: *In the U.S.*: 3010 Walden Avenue, P.O. Box 9077, Buffalo, NY 14269-9077; *In Canada*: P.O. Box 636, Fort Erie, Ontario, L2A 5X3.

Name: _____

Address: _____ City: _____

State/Prov.: _____ Zip/Postal Code: _____

*New York residents remit applicable sales taxes.
Canadian residents remit applicable GST and provincial taxes.

SBACK-OD